INTRODUCING
ISSUES WITH
OPPOSING
VIEWPOINTS®

Women's Rights

Lauri S. Friedman, *Book Editor*

GREENHAVEN PRESS
A part of Gale, Cengage Learning

GALE
CENGAGE Learning

Detroit • New York • San Francisco • New Haven, Conn • Waterville, Maine • London

Christine Nasso, *Publisher*
Elizabeth Des Chenes, *Managing Editor*

© 2010 Greenhaven Press, a part of Gale, Cengage Learning

For more information, contact:
Greenhaven Press
27500 Drake Rd.
Farmington Hills, MI 48331-3535
Or you can visit our Internet site at gale.cengage.com

Articles in Greenhaven Press anthologies are often edited for length to meet page requirements. In addition, original titles of these works are changed to clearly present the main thesis and to explicitly indicate the author's opinion. Every effort is made to ensure that Greenhaven Press accurately reflects the original intent of the authors. Every effort has been made to trace the owners of copyrighted material.

Cover image © Tim Boyle/Getty Images.

LIBRARY OF CONGRESS CATALOGING-IN-PUBLICATION DATA

Women's rights / Lauri S. Friedman, editor.
    p. cm. -- (Introducing issues with opposing viewpoints)
 Includes bibliographical references and index.
 ISBN 978-0-7377-4486-6 (hardcover)
 1. Women's rights--Juvenile literature. I. Friedman, Lauri S.
 HQ1236.W652526 2009
 305.48'697--dc22
 	
                                                                          2009025866

Printed in the United States of America
1 2 3 4 5 6 7 13 12 11 10 09

Contents

Foreword   5

Introduction   7

Chapter 1: What Is the Status of Women's Rights?

1. Women Are Paid Less than Men   11
   Judy Goldberg Dey and Catherine Hill

2. Women Are Not Paid Less than Men   18
   Steve Chapman

3. Women Face Severe Barriers in Politics   24
   Vivian Gornick

4. Women No Longer Face Severe Barriers in Politics   30
   Magnus Linklater

Chapter 2: Does Islam Respect Women's Rights?

1. Islam Respects Women's Rights   37
   Jill Carroll

2. Islam Does Not Respect Women's Rights   43
   Riffat Hassan

3. Violence Against Women in the Name of Islam Is Not Islamic   50
   Harris Zafar

4. The Veil Protects Women's Rights   55
   Yvonne Ridley

5. The Veil Violates Women's Rights   62
   Danielle Crittenden

6. Islam Condemns Honor Killings   69
   Melissa Robinson

7. Islam Condones Honor Killings   75
   Robert Spencer

Chapter 3: What Reproductive Rights Should Women Have?

1. Abortion Is a Woman's Right   82
   Ann Furedi

2. Abortion Is Not a Woman's Right   90
   Randy Alcorn

3. Women Should Have to Consider Men's Feelings
   When Considering Abortion   96
   Courtney E. Martin

4. Women Should Not Have to Consider Men's Feelings
   When Considering Abortion   102
   Catherine Price

5. Women Have a Right to Access Birth Control   107
   Sarah Carey

6. Women Should Not Always Have a Right to Access
   Birth Control   115
   Jay Johansen

Facts About Women's Rights   121
Organizations to Contact   127
For Further Reading   132
Index   137
Picture Credits   142

Foreword

Indulging in a wide spectrum of ideas, beliefs, and perspectives is a critical cornerstone of democracy. After all, it is often debates over differences of opinion, such as whether to legalize abortion, how to treat prisoners, or when to enact the death penalty, that shape our society and drive it forward. Such diversity of thought is frequently regarded as the hallmark of a healthy and civilized culture. As the Reverend Clifford Schutjer of the First Congregational Church in Mansfield, Ohio, declared in a 2001 sermon, "Surrounding oneself with only like-minded people, restricting what we listen to or read only to what we find agreeable is irresponsible. Refusing to entertain doubts once we make up our minds is a subtle but deadly form of arrogance." With this advice in mind, Introducing Issues with Opposing Viewpoints books aim to open readers' minds to the critically divergent views that comprise our world's most important debates.

Introducing Issues with Opposing Viewpoints simplifies for students the enormous and often overwhelming mass of material now available via print and electronic media. Collected in every volume is an array of opinions that captures the essence of a particular controversy or topic. Introducing Issues with Opposing Viewpoints books embody the spirit of nineteenth-century journalist Charles A. Dana's axiom: "Fight for your opinions, but do not believe that they contain the whole truth, or the only truth." Absorbing such contrasting opinions teaches students to analyze the strength of an argument and compare it to its opposition. From this process readers can inform and strengthen their own opinions, or be exposed to new information that will change their minds. Introducing Issues with Opposing Viewpoints is a mosaic of different voices. The authors are statesmen, pundits, academics, journalists, corporations, and ordinary people who have felt compelled to share their experiences and ideas in a public forum. Their words have been collected from newspapers, journals, books, speeches, interviews, and the Internet, the fastest growing body of opinionated material in the world.

Introducing Issues with Opposing Viewpoints shares many of the well-known features of its critically acclaimed parent series, Opposing Viewpoints. The articles are presented in a pro/con format, allowing readers to absorb divergent perspectives side by side. Active reading questions preface each viewpoint, requiring the student to approach the material thoughtfully and carefully. Useful charts, graphs, and cartoons supplement each article. A thorough introduction provides readers with crucial background on an issue. An annotated bibliography points the reader toward articles, books, and Web sites that contain additional information on the topic. An appendix of organizations to contact contains a wide variety of charities, nonprofit organizations, political groups, and private enterprises that each hold a position on the issue at hand. Finally, a comprehensive index allows readers to locate content quickly and efficiently.

Introducing Issues with Opposing Viewpoints is also significantly different from Opposing Viewpoints. As the series title implies, its presentation will help introduce students to the concept of opposing viewpoints and learn to use this material to aid in critical writing and debate. The series' four-color, accessible format makes the books attractive and inviting to readers of all levels. In addition, each viewpoint has been carefully edited to maximize a reader's understanding of the content. Short but thorough viewpoints capture the essence of an argument. A substantial, thought-provoking essay question placed at the end of each viewpoint asks the student to further investigate the issues raised in the viewpoint, compare and contrast two authors' arguments, or consider how one might go about forming an opinion on the topic at hand. Each viewpoint contains sidebars that include at-a-glance information and handy statistics. A Facts About section located in the back of the book further supplies students with relevant facts and figures.

Following in the tradition of the Opposing Viewpoints series, Greenhaven Press continues to provide readers with invaluable exposure to the controversial issues that shape our world. As John Stuart Mill once wrote: "The only way in which a human being can make some approach to knowing the whole of a subject is by hearing what can be said about it by persons of every variety of opinion and studying all modes in which it can be looked at by every character of mind. No wise man ever acquired his wisdom in any mode but this." It is to this principle that Introducing Issues with Opposing Viewpoints books are dedicated.

Introduction

The status of women's rights varies from country to country. Whereas women in some areas of the world are focusing on getting equal pay for equal work, others are petitioning for the right to stay home—or not stay home—with their children. Some women seek greater representation in business and politics, and others pursue equal opportunities in health care and education. In some parts of the world, however, women are fighting a particularly horrifying practice known as female genital mutilation, which the World Health Organization and numerous other groups have called a violation of women's human rights and an extreme form of discrimination against them.

Female genital mutilation (FGM) is a procedure in which a girl's or woman's external genitals are cut, scarred, or partially or entirely removed. It is incredibly painful and can cause a woman to go into shock, bleed profusely, and become prone to infections or sores. It also prevents her from experiencing any sexual pleasure and, in some cases, from having children.

FGM is most commonly practiced in the western, eastern, and northeastern areas of Africa—surveys show it is practiced in at least twenty-eight countries on that continent. Women also undergo the procedure in some Asian and Middle Eastern countries, and among some immigrant communities in the United States and Europe. It is usually carried out on young girls between infancy and age fifteen (occasionally it is performed on grown women) by a tribal medical practitioner who also practices circumcision.

The World Health Organization estimates that between 100 million and 140 million girls and women worldwide have undergone some form of female genital mutilation. Africa is home to the highest number of females living with the consequences of FGM—on that continent alone there are believed to be more than 92 million girls older than age nine who have undergone the procedure, and another 3 million are at risk for it every year.

Communities that practice FGM do so for several reasons. Some societies believe female genital mutilation is necessary in order to properly raise a girl. Others believe it is an important rite of passage that prepares women for marriage and adulthood. Some cultures do it to put limits on the sexuality of their girls—if girls are unable to feel sexual pleasure, it is believed they will be more likely to be faithful to their future husbands. In fact, in some cultures, men will only marry women who have had their genitals mutilated. Other cultures mistakenly believe that a woman who has undergone FGM will always stay a virgin. Finally, some cultures believe that FGM makes girls more attractive as it gives their genitals a smooth look and is said to enhance a man's sexual pleasure.

Interestingly, in cultures where FGM is practiced, it is usually supported by both men and women. Experts say girls may want to undergo the procedure to fit in or to avoid being rejected by their family and friends. Other studies have found that girls may want to undergo the procedure to prevent being ostracized from their community and to be able to find a husband willing to marry them.

But even if girls willingly undergo the procedure, it is not one they enjoy. "I was genitally mutilated at the age of ten," remembers Hannah Koroma, a girl from Sierra Leone. "The pain was terrible and unbearable. . . . I was badly cut and lost blood. . . . I was genitally mutilated with a blunt penknife. . . . Sometimes I had to force myself not to urinate for fear of the terrible pain. I was not given any anesthetic in the operation to reduce my pain, nor any antibiotics to fight against infection."[1] Koroma is one of millions of girls who have undergone this irrevocable procedure in nations such as Chad, Egypt, Ethiopia, Ghana, Kenya, Niger, Sudan, Yemen, and many others. In some of these nations, the United Nations Children's Fund (UNICEF) estimates that the prevalence of girls and women who have been genitally mutilated is more than 90 percent of the female population.

A multitude of international organizations, including the Office of the High Commissioner for Human Rights; the United Nations Development Programme; Amnesty International; Human Rights Watch; the United Nations Educational, Scientific, and Cultural Organization; and the United Nations Development Fund for Women, have denounced female genital mutilation as a barbaric violation of women's rights. "FGM is recognized internationally as a violation of the human rights of girls and women," states the World Health Organization.

It reflects deep-rooted inequality between the sexes, and constitutes an extreme form of discrimination against women. It is nearly always carried out on minors and is a violation of the rights of children. The practice also violates a person's rights to health, security and physical integrity, the right to be free from torture and cruel, inhuman or degrading treatment, and the right to life when the procedure results in death.[2]

Some progress is being made in curbing this disturbing practice. In April 2009, for example, ten villages in western Niger publicly denounced the practice of female genital mutilation and called for all people living in the region to stop performing it. One practitioner, Kompoa Tamkpa, explained she had stopped performing the procedure because she realized it was hurting women. "I have given up the bad work, because it does not bring anything to our village," she said. "We thought it was good for women, that it was going to bring them success. But we found out that it does not bring anything."[3] In Niger, efforts by UNICEF and other organizations have resulted in the rate of genital mutilation dropping by more than half between 1998 and 2006. But about 66 percent of women in the west of the country are still believed to undergo the procedure.

Reducing the number of women who are genitally mutilated is just one of the many forms women's rights battles can take. Others—such as receiving equal pay for equal work, being equally represented in schools and professions, having adequate access to health care, voting rights, and political representation—have a place on women's rights agendas in almost every nation in the world. These and other women's issues are discussed in *Introducing Issues with Opposing Viewpoints: Women's Rights.* The wealth of information and perspectives provided in the article pairs will help readers come to their own conclusions about the status of women's rights in the United States and other nations.

Notes

1. Quoted in Amnesty International USA, "Female Genital Mutilation: A Fact Sheet," 2009.
2. World Health Organization, "Female Genital Mutilation," Fact Sheet No. 241, May 2008.
3. Quoted in CNN.com, "African Villages Denounce Female Circumcision," April 15, 2009.

Chapter 1

What Is the Status of Women's Rights?

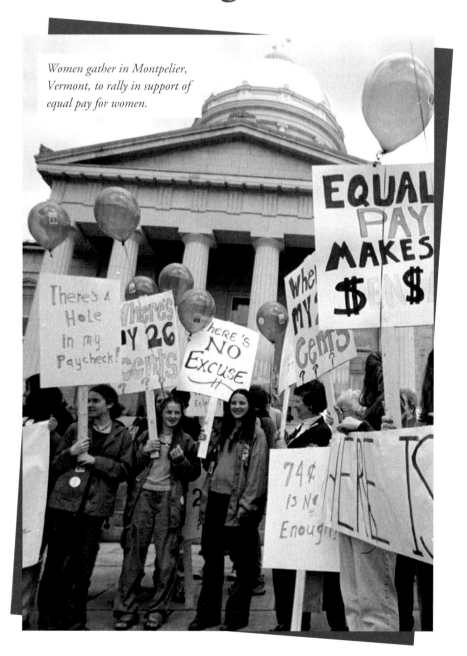

Women gather in Montpelier, Vermont, to rally in support of equal pay for women.

Viewpoint

1

Women Are Paid Less than Men

Judy Goldberg Dey and Catherine Hill

"The gender pay gap has become a fixture of the U.S. workplace and is so ubiquitous that many simply view it as normal."

In the following viewpoint Judy Goldberg Dey and Catherine Hill argue it is an injustice that women continue to be paid less than men for working the same jobs. They explain that women are often pushed into lower-paying fields or are forced to be the primary caregiver for their children, which limits the amount of time they spend in the workforce. But even when women earn the same degrees as men, enter the same fields, and even hold the same positions, Dey and Hill claim they are paid less and are given inferior working conditions. The authors argue that although women have made many gains in recent decades, society will not be equal until women are paid equally for their work.

Judy Goldberg Dey and Catherine Hill are associated with the American Association of University Women Educational Foundation, a nonprofit advocate of equality and education for girls and women.

AS YOU READ, CONSIDER THE FOLLOWING QUESTIONS:
1. According to the authors, how much less do women earn than men ten years after graduating from college?
2. How do male and female salaries compare in the field of education, according to Dey and Hill?
3. What percent of mothers do the authors say were out of the workforce in 2003? What percent of fathers were out of the workforce?

W omen have made remarkable gains in education during the past three decades, yet these achievements have resulted in only modest improvements in pay equity. The gender pay gap has become a fixture of the U.S. workplace and is so ubiquitous that many simply view it as normal. . . .

Women Still Earn Less

One year out of college, women working full time earn only 80 percent as much as their male colleagues earn. Ten years after graduation, women fall farther behind, earning only 69 percent as much as men earn. Controlling for hours, occupation, parenthood, and other factors normally associated with pay, college-educated women still earn less than their male peers earn.

Individuals can, however, make choices that can greatly enhance their earnings potential. Choosing to attend college and completing a college degree have strong positive effects on earnings, although all college degrees do not have the same effect. The selectivity of the college attended and the choice of a major also affect later earnings. Many majors remain strongly dominated by one gender. Female students are concentrated in fields associated with lower earnings, such as education, health, and psychology. Male students dominate the higher-paying fields: engineering, mathematics, and physical sciences. Women and men who majored in "male-dominated" subjects earn more than do those who majored in "female-dominated" or "mixed-gender" fields. For example, one year after graduation, the average female education major working full time earns only 60 percent as much as the average female engineering major working full time earns.

The choice of major is not the full story, however. As early as one year after graduation, a pay gap is found between women and men who had the same college major. In education, a female-dominated major, women earn 95 percent as much as their male colleagues earn. In biological sciences, a mixed-gender major, women earn only 75 percent as much as men earn. Likewise in mathematics—a male-dominated major—women earn only 76 percent as much as men earn. Female students cannot simply choose a major that will allow them to avoid the pay gap.

Burden of Child Care Falls on Mothers

Early career choices, most prominently occupational choices, also play a role in the gender pay gap. While the choice of major is related to occupation, the relationship is not strict. For example, some mathematics majors choose to teach, while others work in business or computer science. One year after graduation, women who work in

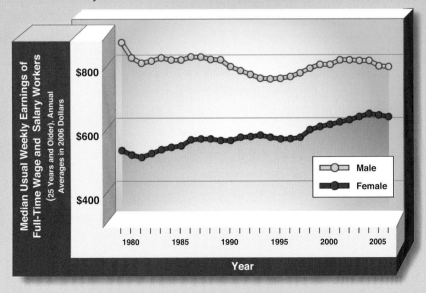

Women Earn Less than Men

Women continue to earn substantially less than their male counterparts—about seventy-seven cents to every male-earned dollar.

Taken from: Judy Goldberg Dey and Catherine Hill, *Behind the Pay Gap*, Washington, DC: American Association of University Women Educational Foundation, 2007.

computer science, for instance, earn over 37 percent more than do women who are employed in education or administrative, clerical, or legal support occupations. Job sector also affects earnings. Women are more likely than men to work in the nonprofit and local government sectors, where wages are typically lower than those in the for-profit and federal government sectors.

The division of labor between parents appears to be similar to that of previous generations. Motherhood and fatherhood affect careers differently. Mothers are more likely than fathers (or other women) to work part time, take leave, or take a break from the work force—factors that negatively affect wages. Among women who graduated from college in 1992–93, more than one-fifth (23 percent) of mothers were out of the work force in 2003, and another 17 percent were working part time. Less than 2 percent of fathers were out of the work force in 2003, and less than 2 percent were working part time. On average, mothers earn less than women without children earn, and both groups earn less than men earn.

Fast Fact

The U.S. Department of Labor reported in 2007 that whereas the median annual income for female full-time workers was $35,102, men earned $45,113.

The gender pay gap among full-time workers understates the real difference between women's and men's earnings because it excludes women who are not in the labor force or who are working part time. Most college-educated women who are not working full time will eventually return to the full-time labor market. On average, these women will then have lower wages than will their continuously employed counterparts, further widening the pay gap.

The Pay Gap Is *Not* About Different Choices

What can be done about the gender pay gap? To begin with, it must be publicly recognized as a problem. Too often, both women and men dismiss the pay gap as simply a matter of different choices, but even women who make the same occupational choices that men make will not typically end up with the same earnings. Moreover, if "too

Motherhood and fatherhood affect careers differently. Mothers are more likely than fathers to work part-time or take a leave from the workplace.

many" women make the same choice, earnings in that occupation can be expected to decline overall.

Women's personal choices are similarly fraught with inequities. The difference between motherhood and fatherhood is particularly stark. Motherhood in our society entails substantial economic and personal sacrifices. Fatherhood, on the other hand, appears to engender a "wage premium." Indeed, men appear to spend *more* time at the office after becoming a father, whereas women spend considerably less time at work after becoming a mother. Women who do not have children may still be viewed as "potential mothers" by employers, who may, as a result, give women fewer professional opportunities.

Men and Women Should Be Treated Equally

Ideally, women and men should have similar economic opportunities and equal opportunities to enjoy meaningful unpaid work, such as parenting. Improving women's earnings could have positive consequences for men who would like to spend more time with their children but who can't afford to reduce their work hours. Likewise, workplace accommodations for parenting could be valuable for fathers as well as mothers. Other groups may also benefit from greater flexibility in the workplace, including older workers seeking "partial retirement," students hoping to combine work with study, and workers with other kinds of caregiving responsibilities.

The pay gap between female and male college graduates cannot be fully accounted for by factors known to affect wages, such as experience (including work hours), training, education, and personal characteristics. Gender pay discrimination can be overt or it can be subtle. It is difficult to document because someone's gender is usually easily identified by name, voice, or appearance. The only way to discover discrimination is to eliminate the other possible explanations. In this analysis the portion of the pay gap that remains unexplained after all other factors are taken into account is 5 percent one year after graduation and 12 percent 10 years after graduation. These unexplained gaps are evidence of discrimination, which remains a serious problem for women in the work force.

Let's Make Equality a Reality

Women's progress throughout the past 30 years attests to the possibility of change. Before Title VII of the Civil Rights Act of 1964[1] and Title IX of the Education Amendments of 1972,[2] employers could— and did—refuse to hire women for occupations deemed "unsuitable,"

1. Title VII made it illegal for employers to discriminate on the basis of gender.
2. Title IX made it illegal for any education program or activity to discriminate on the basis of gender.

fire women when they became pregnant, or limit women's work schedules on the basis of gender. Schools could—and did—set quotas for the number of women admitted or refuse women admission altogether. In the decades since these civil rights laws were enacted, women have made remarkable progress in fields such as law, medicine, and business as well as some progress in nontraditional "blue-collar" jobs such as aviation and firefighting.

Despite the progress women have made, gender pay equity in the workplace remains an issue. Improvements to federal equal pay laws are needed to ensure that women and men are compensated fairly when they perform the same or comparable work. Flexibility, meaningful part-time work opportunities, and expanded provisions for medical and family leave are important to help women and men better balance work and family responsibilities. Making gender pay equity a reality will require action by individuals, employers, and federal and state governments.

EVALUATING THE AUTHORS' ARGUMENTS:

The authors rely on several statistics to make their argument that women earn less than men. Explain which of these statistics most compelled you to agree with their argument. Why? Which of these statistics did you find least compelling? Why?

Women Are Not Paid Less than Men

Steve Chapman

"The pay disparity caused by ... choices [made by women] can't be blamed on piggish employers."

In the following viewpoint Steve Chapman argues that women are not paid less than men. If women earn less than men, Chapman says, it is because they choose to enter lower-paying fields. Furthermore, according to Chapman, women choose to work fewer hours than men and to remove themselves from the workforce in order to raise children. These choices might result in lower salaries, but in Chapman's opinion, it cannot be fairly said that women are not paid equally for the same job performance. He concludes that it is the professional choices men and women make that determine the difference in their salaries, not a discriminatory society.

Steve Chapman is a columnist and an editorial writer for the *Chicago Tribune*.

AS YOU READ, CONSIDER THE FOLLOWING QUESTIONS:
1. According to Chapman, how many more hours a week do men work than women?
2. What can three-quarters of the wage gap be attributed to, according to the author?
3. Who is Claudia Golden? How does the author factor her into his argument?

N ew Year's Day is called that because it begins a new year, and Thanksgiving has that name because it's an occasion for expressing gratitude. But Equal Pay Day, observed this year on April 24, is named for something that, we are told, doesn't exist—equal pay for men and women.

It Is Not Clear the Pay Gap Even Exists

The National Committee on Pay Equity used the occasion to announce that among full-time workers, women make only 77 cents for every dollar paid to men. . . .

And the effort got new fuel from a report by the American Association of University Women (AAUW) Educational Foundation, which says women are paid less starting with their first jobs out of

In the viewpoint the author asserts that women choose to raise children or work part-time, and as a result, they earn less over time than men.

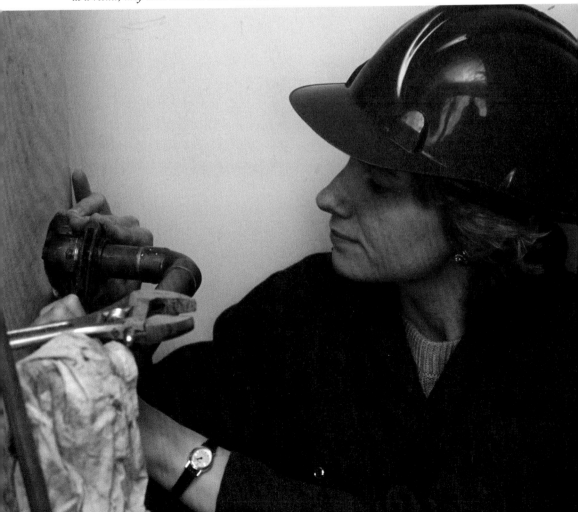

college, and that the deficit only grows with time. Pay discrimination, says AAUW, is still "a serious problem for women in the work force."

In reality, that's not clear at all. What we know from an array of evidence, including this report, is that most if not all of the discrepancy can be traced to factors other than sexism. When it comes to pay equity, we really have come a long way.

Women Choose Career Fields That Pay Less

On its face, the evidence in the AAUW study looks damning. "One year out of college," it says, "women working full-time earn only 80 percent as much as their male colleagues earn. Ten years after graduation, women fall farther behind, earning only 69 percent as much as men earn."

FAST FACT

According to Linda Babcock and Sara Laschever, authors of *Women Don't Ask: Negotiation and the Gender Divide,* men negotiate with their employers for more money four times more often than women do. When women do negotiate, they tend to ask for about 30 percent less than men do.

But read more, and you learn things that don't get much notice on Equal Pay Day. As the report acknowledges, women with college degrees tend to go into fields like education, psychology and the humanities, which typically pay less than the sectors preferred by men, such as engineering, math and business. They are also more likely than men to work for non-profit groups and local governments, which do not offer salaries that [major league baseball player] Alex Rodriguez would envy.

Women Choose to Raise Their Children and Work Less

As they get older, many women elect to work less so they can spend time with their children. A decade after graduation, 39 percent of women are out of the work force or working part time—compared with only 3 percent of men. When these mothers return to full-time jobs, they naturally earn less than they would have if they had never left.

Even before they have kids, men and women often do different things that may affect earnings. A year out of college, notes AAUW,

Women Choose Different Career Paths than Men

Women hold fewer managerial and administrative positions than men do. Some say this is why they earn less than men—because they choose different jobs, not because there is a wage gap.

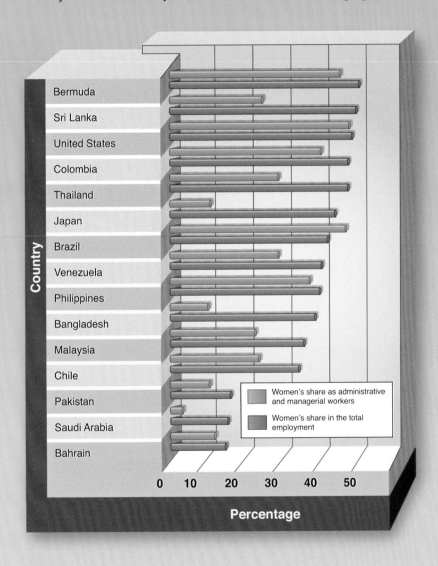

Taken from: International Labor Organization 2003, *Yearbook of Labor Statistics*, Countries with ISCO-1968 classifications. Major group 2.

women in full-time jobs work an average of 42 hours a week, compared to 45 for men. Men are also far more likely to work more than 50 hours a week.

Other Factors Account for Differences in Pay

Buried in the report is a startling admission: "After accounting for all factors known to affect wages, about one-quarter of the gap remains unexplained and *may* be attributed to discrimination" (my emphasis). Another way to put it is that three-quarters of the gap clearly has innocent causes—and that we actually don't know whether discrimination accounts for the rest.

I asked Harvard economist Claudia Goldin if there is sufficient evidence to conclude that women experience systematic pay discrimination. "No," she replied. There are certainly instances of discrimination, she says, but most of the gap is the result of different choices. Other hard-to-measure factors, Goldin thinks, largely account for the remaining gap—"probably not all, but most of it."

The divergent career paths of men and women may reflect a basic unfairness in what's expected of them. It could be that a lot of mothers, if they had their way, would rather pursue careers but have to stay home with the kids because their husbands insist. Or it may be that for one reason or another, many mothers prefer to take on the lion's share of child-rearing. In any case, the pay disparity caused by these choices can't be blamed on piggish employers.

We Are Close to True Equality

June O'Neill, an economist at Baruch College and former director of the Congressional Budget Office, has uncovered something that debunks the discrimination thesis. Take out the effects of marriage and child-rearing, and the difference between the genders suddenly vanishes. "For men and women who never marry and never have children, there is no earnings gap," she said in an interview.

That's a fact you won't hear from AAUW or the Democratic presidential candidates. The prevailing impulse on Equal Pay Day was to lament how far we are from the goal. The true revelation, though, is how close.

EVALUATING THE AUTHORS' ARGUMENTS:

Both Steve Chapman and Judy Goldberg Dey and Catherine Hill, authors of the previous viewpoint, discuss the role choice plays in the pay gap. Chapman argues that women are paid less as a result of choices they make regarding the fields they enter and the time they take off to raise children; Dey and Hill disagree. After reading both viewpoints, with which perspective do you agree? To what extent do you think choice influences the amount men and women are paid?

Women Face Severe Barriers in Politics

Vivian Gornick

"*The degree to which this trashing [of Hillary Rodham Clinton] persisted administered a shock to the system of anyone who wanted to believe that simple woman-hating was a thing of the near past.*"

Vivian Gornick is the author of *The Solitude of Self: Thinking About Elizabeth Cady Stanton* and *The Men in My Life.* In the following viewpoint she uses the example of the 2008 presidential election to argue that women still face severe barriers in politics. She discusses how Hillary Rodham Clinton, who ran for president, was criticized not for her policies but for her hair, figure, demeanor, and appearance. On the other hand, Gornick says, Sarah Palin, the Republican vice presidential nominee, was grossly unqualified for the position and put on the ballot simply *because* she was a woman. Although Gornick appreciates the fact that women were involved so heavily in the presidential campaign, she thinks the way in which these women were treated and selected for candidacy indicates how far women have yet to come in American politics.

1. What sexist T-shirts were made popular by the 2008 campaign of Hillary Rodham Clinton, as reported by the author?
2. According to Gornick, why was the nomination of Sarah Palin for vice president evidence of sexism?
3. What does the term *Pandora's box* mean in the context of the viewpoint?

For a second-wave feminist like myself, this election year [2008] has been a roller-coaster ride: exciting, and sick-making, and yet again exciting. We have seen an eminently qualified woman [Hillary Rodham Clinton] contend for a presidential nomination and fail, at least in part because she was demonized as a dragon lady; then we have seen a shamefully unqualified woman [Alaska governor Sarah Palin] handed a vice presidential nomination, at least in part because she was a walking advertisement for Mrs. America. Taken together, such unforeseen events have been remarkable, especially insofar as they remind us of where we are, as a culture, in the centuries-long struggle to normalize equality for women.

Proof in 2008 That Sexism Lives On

The second wave of American feminism is now in a period of quietude, even of setback. After nearly 40 years of noisy activity on behalf of women's rights, a large part of the country thinks the revolution's been won, another large part thinks what feminists have accomplished amounts to a drop in the bucket, and yet a third part remains irredeemably opposed to feminist values. Such an extraordinary division of viewpoint indicates that whatever the gains for women have been, they are by no means indisputable, much less guaranteed a lasting life.

An incontestable piece of evidence that high-level sexism persists in the United States was the astonishing treatment meted out to Hillary Rodham Clinton throughout her tortured campaign to win the Democratic Party's nomination for president. She was trashed all over the country—in the papers, on television and on the Internet—solely, repeatedly, insultingly, not as a Washington insider, or as a senator who endorsed the Iraq war, or as a member of a would-be political dynasty, but as a woman.

An Unequal World

A 2008 poll revealed that many Americans believe women do not receive equal treatment in many areas of life, and particularly in politics.

Question: Thinking about how the world actually works, do you think women in the United States are treated equally...

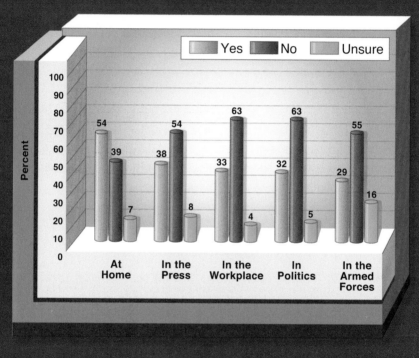

Taken from: Penn, Schoen & Berland Associates, November 5–6, 2008.

Woman-Hating Is Alive and Well

She was routinely characterized as strident and aggressive; criticized on her hair, her clothing, her figure; called an uppity woman on television; and on the Internet one could see a notice that read, "The bitch is back '08," as well as a video of a man at a rally screaming at Clinton, "Iron my shirt."

The degree to which this trashing persisted administered a shock to the system of anyone who wanted to believe that simple woman-hating was a thing of the near past. It is painful and instructive to realize that it was unthinkable to level equivalent open racism at [then presidential candidate] Barack Obama. Obviously, if you were so inclined, you could think racist thoughts, but you could not speak them; whereas, with sexism, it was no holds barred.

Another indisputable piece of evidence that sexism is still very much with us was the nomination of Sarah Palin for vice president on the Republican ticket: a piece of cynicism that was truly an insult to all of us, women and men alike. Palin was chosen, with an ugly wink at the country, because she was a sexy, cheerleading fundamentalist. It was as though the conservatives felt free to say, "You want a woman? We'll give you a woman"—as they trotted out a parody of American politics that could have been invented by [novelist] Thomas Pynchon.

Feminists Have More Work to Do

At the same time, it has been thrilling to see thousands upon thousands of women (and men too) rise up in righteous anger against the sexism inherent in both Clinton's defeat and Palin's ascent. The twin event has politicized people who, until that moment, did not think they had feminist politics. The spectacular protest is a true measure of how far American feminism has actually come—how much deeper it has penetrated the shared sensibility of the body politic than we have generally realized—and how far it has yet to go. This aspect of a hardly credible election year has been a joy and a high for many of us, and a salutary reminder that the struggle over women's rights remains one of the longest and most resilient on human record.

> **FAST FACT**
>
> A woman has never been elected to the office of the president of the United States. Forty-four men have served as president from 1789 to 2009.

The modern women's movement dates from the 1792 publication of [writer] Mary Wollstonecraft's "Vindication of the Rights of Woman." Written in the wake of the French Revolution, this remarkably radical treatise posits that women need to use their minds more than they need to be mothers and wives, in the same way that men need to use their minds more than they need to be fathers and husbands. Not instead of, just more than.

Every 50 years since that time, the movement has raised its head, opened its mouth, made yet another effort to have that sentiment heard, absorbed and acted on. Each time around, its partisans have been renamed—new women, odd women, free women, liberated women—but in actuality, they are always the same women. And, while they have had different issues to take up—the right to vote, or divorce, own property, go to medical school—their underlying message has always been the same: The conviction that men by nature take their brains seriously, and women by nature do not, is based not on an inborn reality but on a cultural belief that has served our deepest insecurities. That is the real issue, and around it there has collected over these two centuries a great amount of thought and feeling, and an even greater amount of anxiety, in women and men alike.

The author says that during the 2008 presidential campaign Hillary Clinton was criticized for her hair, figure, and clothing in a way a male candidate would not have been.

Women Have More Barriers to Break in Politics

It is, I think, safe to say that the question of equality for women, each and every time around, has opened a Pandora's box of fear, hope and confusion that is existential in its very nature and has made its resolution even more recalcitrant than the matter of equality for people of color. In short: Behind the idea that it is natural for women to take an equal part in the world-making enterprise lies an internal self-division—a conflict of social will—that, at this moment, is far from clarified. Someday, perhaps, it will be, but today is not that day.

However, an election year such as we have just had in the United States should make every feminist in the country eager to press on.

> ### EVALUATING THE AUTHOR'S ARGUMENTS:
>
> Gornick explains that Hillary Rodham Clinton and Sarah Palin are two very different women—yet each of their experiences running for office in 2008 demonstrated different aspects of sexism. Do you agree with her on this point? Why or why not? Use evidence from the viewpoint in your answer.

Viewpoint

4

Women No Longer Face Severe Barriers in Politics

Magnus Linklater

"It may be that women, far from being trapped beneath a glass ceiling, have wisely decided to ignore it altogether."

In the following viewpoint, Scottish author Magnus Linklater argues that women no longer face severe barriers in politics. He points out that women now hold top positions in almost all professional and political organizations—women govern cities; head important councils; act as legal and educational leaders; run boardrooms, banks, parliaments, universities, and military operations all over the world. In Linklater's opinion, it is difficult to claim that women face severe barriers when they have achieved so much. In areas where women have not achieved as much as men, Linklater explains it is because women have made different career choices, choosing to embrace a more satisfying but less ambitious job, for example. Linklater urges members of society to stop acting as if there is some sort of glass ceiling that women are unable to break through and accept the fact that women are no longer discriminated against in politics or other fields.

Magnus Linklater is a Scottish journalist and a former newspaper editor.

Magnus Linklater, "Concept of a Glass Ceiling for Women Not as Clear as It First Appears," *The Scotsman,* January 7, 2007. Reproduced by permission.

AS YOU READ, CONSIDER THE FOLLOWING QUESTIONS:

1. Why is the author skeptical of claims made by the Equal Opportunities Commission that women continue to face prejudice in politics?
2. How does the author explain the relative absence of women from top jobs?
3. What does the term *status-conscious* mean in the context of the viewpoint?

What is all this talk about a glass ceiling—or even, as the new woman speaker of the US House of Representatives [Nancy Pelosi] called it last week, a "marble ceiling?" It has been splintered so often now I am beginning to wonder whether it exists at all. Perhaps it is like the emperor's new clothes—more real in the imagination than in fact. We look around Scotland and see women running our cities, our councils, our legal profession and our education authorities; we find them on boardrooms and in banks. They are on the front benches of our parliament, leading two of our political parties, acting as Lords Lieutenant, heading up universities and financial institutions, even, for heaven's sake, being appointed Yeomen of the Guard and exported south to defend the Tower of London. And still we talk about glass ceilings. At least let's smash the cliché, even if we can't avoid the argument.

Equality Organizations Are Self-Serving

The complainers, I notice, are usually organisations such as the Equal Opportunities Commission [EOC], which has a vested interest in promoting the notion of persistent inequality rather than in noting progress made. Its annual report announces, with weary predictability, that hundreds of women are missing from top jobs. There should, it says, be many more female judges, senior police officers, council leaders, company directors and MSPs [members of Scottish Parliament] than there are now. The only thing holding them back is the prejudice of a male-dominated society, and the reluctance of companies to allow women the flexible working hours that would allow them to take time off to look after their children and their homes.

We should recognise two things right away about the EOC. First, that on the day it starts issuing a report saying that women are making excellent progress, taking on a number of top jobs previously held by men and doing very well, thank you, that day it might just as well pronounce itself redundant, losing its healthy subsidy and its well-paid appointments. Secondly, it is about to be absorbed into the new Commission for Equality and Human Rights, which means that its complaints, far from dying away, will now be redoubled. Get ready for many more reports along the same lines—the glass ceiling concept is about to be double-glazed.

Women Have Made Massive Progress

But its claims should be examined with deepest scepticism. Is there really, despite all the massive progress made by women on the job front, despite the legislation which enforces equality, and despite the publicity which surrounds it, a hidden barrier to promotion that operates against women and is holding them back? Are the male bastions

The author asserts that the glass ceiling for women has been broken in many professions, including politics.

of power still jealously guarded and the prejudices of male-dominated organisations still firmly intact? Or is the truth that the feminine approach to work is fundamentally different to that of men?

That the feminine approach cherishes values such as job satisfaction, self-fulfilment, and the worthwhile nature of work rather than the desperate need for advancement which fuels the male ego? A woman executive in a bank, for instance, is more likely to give her attention to the project she is managing, rather than to wonder where the next career change is coming from. She may well find it faintly ridiculous, not to say a waste of valuable time, when she observes the efforts that go into the lobbying for promotion, and the need for status which drives her male counterpart into the boss's office demanding a raise, a larger desk and a longer title.

FAST FACT

In 2008 Alaska governor Sarah Palin became the first woman on a Republican presidential ticket when she ran as Senator John McCain's vice presidential candidate. In 1984 Geraldine Ferraro became the first woman to run on any presidential ticket when Democratic presidential candidate Walter Mondale selected her to be his running mate.

Women Make or Break Their Own Success

To suggest that women create their own barriers to progress, and are often content to do so, is to invite fury and contempt from the campaigners, but after a lifetime in journalism, one of the most male-orientated professions I know, I would say the relative absence of women from the top jobs has less to do with male prejudice than with the different approaches women adopt to the jobs that they are given.

As an editor I was well used to journalists knocking on my door, applying for promotion, asking for salary reviews, and suggesting ways in which their roles could be expanded or enhanced. They were almost always men. They wanted to know who was likely to fill a post that had fallen vacant, to complain that someone doing the same job as them was paid more, or to enquire what plans I had for improving

More Women Enter Politics Every Year

As of 2006, one-fifth of the world's parliamentarians elected in 2005 were women. In nineteen countries women make up more than 30 percent of their parliaments.

Country	Percentage
Rwanda	48.8
Sweden	45.3
Norway	37.9
Finland	37.5
Denmark	36.9
Netherlands	36.7
Cuba	36.0
Spain	36.0
Costa Rica	35.1
Argentina	35.0
Mozambique	34.8
Belgium	34.7
Austria	33.9
Iceland	33.3
South Africa	32.8
New Zealand	32.2
Germany	31.8
Guyana	30.8
Burundi	30.5
Tanzania	30.4

Taken from: Inter-Parliamentary Union, February 2006.

their pay or conditions in view of the excellent contribution they were making to the paper. The women who came in to see me had, by and large, a different agenda. They usually did so to discuss the job itself. They wanted to know how I thought it was working out, to discuss their current approach to it and suggest ways in which it could be done better. They rarely raised the issue of salaries or position.

Let's Not Pretend a Glass Ceiling Exists

I accept that one by-product of this approach was that women's pay frequently lagged behind the general level of their male counterparts. I would also have to admit that, when the top jobs fell vacant, one tended to think of the pushy, demanding male candidates first, rather than the quietly efficient woman who was doing a first-class job and seemed perfectly happy to continue with it. But to describe this as a glass ceiling—an invisible and impenetrable barrier to progress perpetuated by men—seems absurd. What emerges, on the contrary, is a picture of women taking their jobs more seriously and adopting a more mature and responsible approach to them than their aggressive and status-conscious male colleagues.

Sometimes, perhaps, that meant that they were a few rungs lower down the career ladder, but mostly they seemed to derive more satisfaction from their work than the men did. And since, these days, there is less interest in joining the rat race and a greater emphasis on work that offers flexible time, a greater sense of job fulfilment, and the opportunity to improve the quality of life rather than career advancement for its own sake, it may be that women, far from being trapped beneath a glass ceiling, have wisely decided to ignore it altogether.

EVALUATING THE AUTHOR'S ARGUMENTS:

The author of this viewpoint uses the terms *glass ceiling* and *marble ceiling* to make arguments about women in politics. In your own words, describe what you think these terms mean. Then, state whether you agree with the author's opinion of how relevant this glass-ceiling concept actually is to women's status in politics and other fields.

Chapter 2

Does Islam Respect Women's Rights?

A woman demonstrates in Egypt. The rights of Muslim women are hotly debated, and vary from country to country.

Viewpoint
1

Islam Respects Women's Rights

Jill Carroll

"Islamic scholars— from the United States to Yemen— . . . are using religious jurisprudence to argue that women have greater rights under Islam."

Jill Carroll describes the work of Wazhma Frogh, an Afghan woman, in the following viewpoint. Frogh uses religious arguments based on the Koran to show that the Koran does not support the ill treatment of women. Rather, she claims the Koran grants rights to women, and these should be the basis of reform in Muslim nations like Afghanistan. Frogh believes that only religious arguments matter to the people of Afghanistan, so arguments for women's rights are best framed in that context.

AS YOU READ, CONSIDER THE FOLLOWING QUESTIONS:

1. What languages did Frogh speak when quoting verses from the Koran to the mullah in a conservative district in northeastern Afghanistan? Why might she have used those languages?

Jill Carroll, "Inside Islam, a Woman's Roar: Wazhma Frogh, an Afghan, Uses Her Religion to Press for Women's Rights—and Development Agencies Take Note," *The Christian Science Monitor,* March 5, 2008. Copyright © 2008–2009 *The Christian Science Monitor.* All rights reserved. Reproduced by permission from *Christian Science Monitor* (www.csmonitor.com).

2. What is a common type of education for many mullahs in Afghanistan?
3. How did Frogh manage to change her father's opinion of women?

Just hours after Wazhma Frogh arrived in an isolated, conservative district in northeastern Afghanistan in 2002, the local mullah was preaching to his congregation to kill her. Ms. Frogh was meddling with their women with her plan to start a literacy program, he told the assembly.

As she walked past the mosque during noon prayers, his words caught her ear. Shocked, she marched straight into the mosque. In a flowing black chador that left her face uncovered, she strode past the male worshipers and faced the mullah. Trembling inside, she challenged him.

"Mullah, give me five minutes," she recalls saying. "I will tell you something, and after that if you want to say I am an infidel and I am a threat to you, just kill me."

She then rattled off five Koranic verses—in both Arabic and the local Dari language—that extol the virtues of education, tolerance, and not harming others. She criticized local practices of allowing men to use Islam to justify beating their wives, betrothing young girls, and denying women an education.

The room was silent. All eyes were on Frogh and the mullah. Then the mullah rested his hand on her head.

"God bless you, my daughter," he said.

With that, Frogh won permission to start the literacy program that later helped women from Badakhshan Province participate in local government and run for the national assembly.

Where rigid interpretations of Islam relegate women to second-class status, Frogh uses rhetorical jujitsu to turn religious arguments on their heads and win women's rights. Her steely determination has earned her attention in Washington.

"In a country where religion is so important to people, we need to understand the religion," she says. Arguments based on principles of universal human rights or on what international conventions say don't persuade many Afghans to support reforms, she says. "[M]y experience in the last 10 years is this does not matter to the people in Afghanistan," she says. Only religious arguments hold sway.

The international development field has lately seen more of that approach, says Rachel McCleary, a fellow at the Center for International Development at Harvard. In the 1960s and '70s, foreign aid became

Women's Rights in Islam

The Koran lays out a number of rights for women, including:

- The right to respect

- The right to not be enslaved

- The right to inherit property

- The right to justice

- The right to work

- The right to privacy

- The right to divorce

- The right to sustenance

- The right to acquire knowledge

- The right to life

- The right to leave one's homeland if oppressed

- The right to have protection from slander

Compiled by the editor.

Muslim women in Indonesia demonstrate for more rights.

more secularized, but now religious groups are a growing presence in international development work, says Ms. McCleary.

Frogh is like a number of Islamic scholars—from the United States to Yemen—who are using religious jurisprudence to argue that women have greater rights under Islam, convince leaders in Muslim communities to make reforms, or even turn around extremists who use Islam to justify violence. As an Afghan Muslim, Frogh is in the best position to persuade other Afghan Muslims to support her various projects, experts say.

"The fact [that] this woman is from within, and from the culture and society is much more powerful and salient than if a woman from outside said the same thing," says Eileen Babbitt, professor of International Conflict Management Practice at Tufts University's Fletcher School of Law and Diplomacy.

The Power of Religion

Indeed, Frogh believes so deeply in the power of religious arguments to bring reforms, she plans to get a graduate degree related to Islam.

She says many mullahs in Afghanistan are usually only schooled by their fathers, who may be illiterate and not understand the Koran's original Arabic, even if they have memorized it. Her breadth of religious knowledge is key to persuading local religious leaders.

"My goal is to really represent Islam. It's not a religion that oppresses women," Frogh says. "Of course it's very risky. I may lose my life during this process, but if I am able to open a door for rights for one woman, then it is worth it."

She has worked for various humanitarian and development agencies to give women greater rights and education in Afghanistan. Now she works for the Canadian International Development Agency in Afghanistan, consulting on the suitability of projects there, implementing a gender-equity policy, and conducting feasibility studies and other preparations for new projects.

Changing Men's Perceptions

The mullah in Badakhshan Province is one of many men she persuaded to change with regard to their ideas about women. The first was her father. When her wealthy family fled upheaval in Afghanistan in the 1990s for Pakistan, her father, a rigid former Army officer, had a hard time supporting the family.

Frogh, then in eighth grade, thought of a way to help. She offered her landlord's children tutoring in exchange for cheaper rent.

"It made a difference in the way my father perceived me," Frogh says. "He thought women are consumers [who could] never be providers." He even began to consult her on family decisions.

"Because I was able to have that status in the family, it got me thinking. I could be a lawyer and help other people," she recalls. Even as a child, injustice needled her. She resented the fact that women ate in the kitchen while men dined in the living room. Girls swept the yard, but boys played in it.

Her Nation's Future: Hopeful, Tenuous

At the age most American teenagers are learning to drive, Frogh crouched at night on the family's toilet in Pakistan studying English. Only there could she turn on a light without disturbing anyone in their one-room home.

Now, not yet 30, she has President [George W.] Bush's attention. In February she and women from three other countries met with Washington policymakers and aid donors to discuss women and security. The president made a surprise appearance during the group's meeting with the first lady. With her usual directness, Frogh described Afghanistan's future to the president as hopeful but tenuous.

"There is not justice," she recalls telling Mr. Bush. "The Taliban is very much all over the country. Those [who] have violated human rights, they are the ones in the government." Frogh's solution: After her studies, aim high. "I want to be chief justice."

EVALUATING THE AUTHORS' ARGUMENTS:

In this viewpoint, Frogh argues that Islam does not oppress women. Compare this view with the next viewpoint by Riffat Hassan, who argues that some of the current practices in Islamic countries do oppress women. What is the reason for the difference of opinion? Support your answer with evidence from each viewpoint.

Islam Does Not Respect Women's Rights

Riffat Hassan

In the following viewpoint Riffat Hassan argues that Islam does not respect women's rights. Although the Koran, the Muslim holy book, technically grants women the right to get a divorce, the right to inherit property, and the right to acquire an education, Hassan says that most Muslim societies do not uphold these rights. Instead, Hassan says that in many Muslim countries women are the victims of honor killings, infanticide (when girl babies are killed at birth), and female genital mutilation. Furthermore, Muslim men are more concerned with controlling the sexuality of Muslim women than protecting their rights—this is why many are locked away in houses or behind veils, unable to operate freely and equally in society. For all of these reasons, Hassan concludes that Islam in practice does not respect women's rights.

Riffat Hassan is a Pakistani American theologian and a leading Islamic feminist scholar of the Koran. She is a professor of

"Muslim culture has reduced many, if not most, women to the position of puppets on a string, to slave-like creatures whose only purpose in life is to cater to the needs and pleasures of men."

Riffat Hassan, "Are Human Rights Compatible with Islam? The Issue of the Rights of Women in Muslim Communities," The Religious Consultation, accessed March 8, 2009. Reproduced by permission.

religious studies at the University of Louisville, Kentucky, and the founder of the International Network for the Rights of Female Victims of Violence in Pakistan.

AS YOU READ, CONSIDER THE FOLLOWING QUESTIONS:
1. What, according to Hassan, is a common crime in the Muslim nation of Pakistan?
2. A Muslim woman's husband is her gateway to what, according to Hassan?
3. What does the Koran say about a woman's right to divorce? What does Hassan say is practiced in Muslim societies?

Muslim men never tire of repeating that Islam has given more rights to women than has any other religion. Certainly, if by "Islam" is meant "Qur'anic Islam" the rights that it has given to women are, indeed, impressive. Not only do women partake of all the "General Rights" [such as the right to acquire knowledge, divorce, or inherit money], they are also the subject of much particular concern in the Qur'an. Underlying much of the Qu'ran's legislation on women-related issues is the recognition that women have been disadvantaged persons in history to whom justice needs to be done by the Muslim "ummah" [community]. Unfortunately, however, . . . a review of Muslim history and culture brings to light many areas in which—Qur'anic teaching notwithstanding—women continue to be subjected to diverse forms of oppression and injustice, often in the name of Islam, while the Qur'an because of its protective attitude toward all downtrodden and oppressed classes of people, appears to be weighted in many ways in favor of women, many of its women-related teachings have been used in patriarchal Muslim societies against, rather than for, women.

Muslim Cultures Seek Control of a Woman's Body

Muslim societies, in general, appear to be far more concerned with trying to control women's bodies and sexuality than with their human rights. Many Muslims when they speak of human rights, either do not speak of women's rights at all, or are mainly concerned with how a women's chastity may be protected. (They are apparently not worried about protecting men's chastity.)

Women are the targets of the most serious violations of human rights which occur in Muslim societies in general. Muslims say with great pride that Islam abolished female infanticide; true, but, it must also be mentioned that one of the most common crimes in a number

Pakistani women protest the government's reaction to the honor killings of five Pakistani women who were shot and buried alive in August 2008.

of Muslim countries (e.g., in Pakistan) is the murder of women by their husbands. These so-called "honor-killings" are, in fact, extremely dishonorable and are frequently used to camouflage other kinds of crimes.

Females Are Treated as Second-Class Citizens

Female children are discriminated against from the moment of birth, for it is customary in Muslim societies to regard a son as a gift, and a daughter as a trial, from God. Therefore, the birth of a son is an occasion for celebration while the birth of a daughter calls for commiseration if not lamentation. Many girls are married when they are still minors, even though marriage in Islam is a contract and presupposes that the contracting parties are both consenting adults. Even though so much Qur'anic legislation is aimed at protecting the rights of women in the context of marriage women cannot claim equality with their husbands. The husband, in fact, is regarded as his wife's gateway to heaven or hell and the arbiter of her final destiny. That such an idea can exist within the framework of Islam—which, in theory, rejects the idea of there being any intermediary between a believer and God—represents both a profound irony and a great tragedy.

FAST FACT

According to the World Health Organization, 88.5 percent of female genital mutilations—a painful procedure that scars a woman's genitals—have occurred in Muslim nations.

Muslim Women Are Not Truly Granted the Rights Offered in the Qur'an

Although the Qur'an presents the idea of what we today call a "no-fault" divorce and does not make any adverse judgements about divorce, Muslim societies have made divorce extremely difficult for women, both legally and through social penalties. Although the Qur'an states clearly that the divorced parents of a minor child must decide by mutual consultation how the child is to be raised and that they must not use the child to hurt or exploit each other, in most Muslim societies, women are deprived both of their sons (generally at

THIS IS WHAT HAPPENS WHEN A BUNCH OF INSECURE MEN MAKE ALL THE RULES!

caglecartoons.com   courant.com/boblog

"Polygamists and Taliban," cartoon by Bob Englehart, *The Hartford Courant,* April 23, 2008. Copyright © 2008 by Bob Englehart and *The Hartford Courant* and PoliticalCartoons.com. All rights reserved.

age 7) and their daughters (generally at age 12). It is difficult to imagine an act of greater cruelty than depriving a mother of her children simply because she is divorced. Although polygamy was intended by the Qur'an to be for the protection of orphans and widows, in practice Muslims have made it the Sword of Damocles [an ever-present peril] which keeps women under constant threat. Although the Qur'an gave women the right to receive an inheritance not only on the death of a close relative, but also to receive other bequests or gifts during the lifetime of a benevolent caretaker, Muslim societies have disapproved greatly of the idea of giving wealth to a woman in preference to a man, even when her need or circumstances warrant it. Although the purpose of the Qur'anic legislation dealing with women's dress and conduct was to make it safe for women to go about their daily business (since they have the right to engage in gainful activity as witnessed by Surah 4: An-Nisa' :32) without fear of sexual harassment or molestation, Muslim societies have put many of them behind veils and shrouds and locked doors on the pretext of protecting their chastity, forgetting that according to the Qur'an confinement to their homes was not a normal way of life for chaste women but a punishment for "unchastity."

Muslim Societies Subjugate Women

Woman and man, created equal by God and standing equal in the sight of God, have become very unequal in Muslim societies. The Qur'anic description of man and woman in marriage: "They are your garments/And you are their garments" implies closeness, mutuality, and equality. However, Muslim culture has reduced many, if not most, women to the position of puppets on a string, to slave-like creatures whose only purpose in life is to cater to the needs and pleasures of men. Not only this, it has also had the audacity and the arrogance to deny women direct access to God. It is one of Islam's cardinal beliefs that each person—man or woman—is responsible and accountable for his or her individual actions. How, then, can the husband become the wife's gateway to heaven or hell? How, then, can he become the arbiter not only of what happens to her in this world but also of her ultimate destiny? Such questions are now being articulated by an increasing number of Muslim women and they are bound to threaten the existing balance of power in the domain of family relationships in most Muslim societies.

Islam Needs to Reflect and Change

However, despite everything that has gone wrong with the lives of countless Muslim women down the ages due to patriarchal Muslim culture, there is hope for the future. There are indications from across the world of Islam that a growing number of Muslims are beginning to reflect seriously upon the teachings of the Qur'an as they become disenchanted with capitalism, communism and western democracy. As this reflection deepens, it is likely to lead to the realization that the supreme task entrusted to human beings by God, of being God's deputies on earth, can only be accomplished by establishing justice which the Qur'an regards as a prerequisite for authentic peace. Without the elimination of the inequities, inequalities, and injustices that pervade the personal and collective lives of human beings, it is not possible to talk about peace in Qur'anic terms. Here, it is of importance to note that there is more Qur'anic legislation pertaining to the establishment of justice in the context of family relationships than on any other subject. This points to the assumption implicit in much Qur'anic learning, namely, that if human beings can learn to order their homes justly so that the human rights of all within its jurisdiction—children, women, and men—are safeguarded, then they can also order their society, and the world at large, justly. In other words, the Qur'an regards the home as a microcosm of the "ummah" and the world community, and emphasizes the importance of making it "the abode of peace" through just living.

EVALUATING THE AUTHORS' ARGUMENTS:

Both Riffat Hassan and Jill Carroll, author of the previous viewpoint, agree that Islam in theory grants certain rights to women. Yet they disagree on whether Muslim women are able to take advantage of these rights in modern society. After reading both viewpoints, what is your opinion on whether Islam respects women's rights? Explain your answer using evidence from the viewpoints you have read.

Violence Against Women in the Name of Islam Is Not Islamic

Harris Zafar

"The Prophet Muhammad came to give more rights to women; not to take away their rights."

In the following viewpoint, Harris Zafar argues that injustices against women in the name of Islam are not actually Islamic. He describes cases of violence against women in Saudi Arabia, the birthplace of Islam. In one case, a group of unveiled schoolgirls were killed in a fire because Saudi "religious police" would not let them leave the burning building uncovered. In another case, a Saudi teenager who was gang-raped by seven men was forced to serve time in jail: It was decided that she was partially responsible for causing the rape because she left her home unescorted by a male guardian. Zafar says that nowhere in Islam are justifications for these sorts of acts found. He concludes that Islam is a just and peaceful religion that has been co-opted by religious zealots.

Harris Zafar is a business analyst and the president of a youth organization at a Portland, Oregon, mosque.

Harris Zafar, "Justice in Islam: Saudi Outrages Against Women Not Islamic," *Oregonian* (Portland, OR), February 17, 2008, p. E3. Reproduced by permission.

AS YOU READ, CONSIDER THE FOLLOWING QUESTIONS:

1. According to Zafar, what happened to an American business-woman while visiting Saudi Arabia?
2. What percent of the Saudi university students are women, according to Zafar? What percent of Saudi workers are women?
3. What punishment does Zafar say a Saudi teenager received after she was gang-raped by seven men?

I magine this scene: A group of colleagues enters Starbucks to use the wireless Internet. They order coffee, find a table and sit down with their laptops. They are then approached by a mob of men known as the "religious police," who arrest the one woman in the group for sitting with men who are not related to her. In court, instead of being declared guilty or not guilty, she is called a sinner and thrown in jail.

How does this sound? Unrealistic? Well, believe it because this is exactly what happened recently to a U.S. businesswoman in Saudi Arabia who went to a Starbucks with an unrelated male colleague. Though wearing the traditional headscarf and long black coat, she was arrested, strip-searched, forced to sign false confessions and called a sinner.

> **FAST FACT**
>
> The first National Experts Meeting to Fight Domestic Abuse Against Women and Children determined after a two-day conference in May 2008 that there is no justification for abuse of women and children in Islam.

Islam Never Wanted Girls and Women to Die

This is an impractical attempt to force religious practices onto people. Saudi Arabia has become infamous for its religious police (known by the Arabic word "mutaween"), who have the power to arrest unrelated men and women caught socializing; seize products regarded as "un-Islamic"; and enforce Islamic dress codes and dietary laws.

In March 2002, these police forcibly barred schoolgirls from escaping a burning school in Mecca because the girls were not wearing headscarves and black coats. Consequently, 15 girls died and 50 were injured.

A Saudi woman adjusts her veil in a Saudi Arabian shopping mall. Religious police patrol the malls to ensure women follow the strict tenets of Islam.

Last summer, they also arrested and deported every member of the minority Ahmadiyya Muslim Community who were praying in a private residence, simply because they disagreed with the sect's moderate views.

The Homeland of Islam Has Violated the Religion

As a Muslim who understands and follows true Islamic tenets, such cases sadden and infuriate me. The whole idea of "religious police" is absurd. Religion cannot be imposed on anyone. The Holy Quran openly declares in Chapter 2, verse 257: "There shall be no compulsion in religion."

Islam finds its roots in Saudi Arabia. Yet women in that kingdom particularly face discrimination in matters like education, employment and the justice system. Although they make up 70 percent of university enrollment, women comprise just 5 percent of the Saudi work force. They cannot travel abroad, be admitted into a hospital, examined by a doctor or leave the house without permission or company of an immediate male relative.

A Strict, and Wrong, Interpretation of Islamic Law

Women also face discrimination in the Saudi legal system because of the country's strict interpretation of Shariah law.

Recently, seven men abducted a teenage woman with an unrelated man from a mall in Saudi Arabia and raped her. In October [2007], the seven men were sentenced to two to nine years in prison, but the woman was also convicted of breaking the law by not having a male guardian with her and for being alone with an unrelated man. She was sentenced to six months in prison and 200 lashes.

Where is the justice in that? A victim of gang rape, she must face legal punishment?

Islam Has Been Co-Opted and Skewed

Nowhere in Islamic jurisprudence will you find such a rule. This is not Islam. The Prophet Muhammad came to give more rights to women; not to take away their rights. This case drew international outrage, resulting in the woman's pardon by Saudi Arabia's king.

It is so sad to see the definition of justice so skewed in Saudi Arabia. I openly declare that these enemies of justice are not following any Islamic principles related to justice. Islam says that everyone is answerable for their actions to God only. The right to impose religiousness has not been granted to anyone, especially to those who do not even understand the religion.

EVALUATING THE AUTHOR'S ARGUMENTS:

Zafar describes crimes against women that have taken place in Saudi Arabia, the birthplace of Islam. If you were a Muslim, what would you say about such crimes? Would you agree with Zafar that these crimes are not Islamic? Or would you agree with other authors in this chapter that if Muslims commit these crimes, they must be tied somehow to Islam? Explain your reasoning.

Viewpoint

4

The Veil Protects Women's Rights

Yvonne Ridley

"*What is more liberating: being judged on the length of your skirt and the size of your surgically enhanced breasts, or being judged on your character and intelligence?*"

The veil protects and honors women, argues Yvonne Ridley in the following viewpoint. She explains that the veil helps Muslim women be respected and taken seriously by men. In Western cultures, women are forced to use their body to get attention; Ridley says this causes them to dress shamelessly and degrade themselves. But veils help Muslim women be appreciated for more than just their sexual beauty. A veiled woman is respected for the things she says and does, not just by the way she looks, in Ridley's opinion. Furthermore, veiling helps remind men that women are to be respected and cherished. She concludes that the veil is a feminist symbol that offers women self-respect and honor.

Yvonne Ridley is the political editor of Islam Channel TV in London and the coauthor of the book *In the Hands of the Taliban: Her Extraordinary Story.*

AS YOU READ, CONSIDER THE FOLLOWING QUESTIONS:
1. Describe how Ridley was treated after she converted to Islam.
   What kinds of comments did people make to her because she
   was wearing a veil?
2. To which other outfit does the author compare the veil? Why?
3. In what ways does Ridley say Muslim women can be thought of
   as radical feminists?

I used to look at veiled women as quiet, oppressed creatures—until I was captured by the Taliban.

In September 2001, just 15 days after the terrorist attacks on the United States, I snuck into Afghanistan, clad in a head-to-toe blue burqa, intending to write a newspaper account of life under the repressive regime. Instead, I was discovered, arrested and detained for 10 days. I spat and swore at my captors; they called me a "bad" woman but let me go after I promised to read the Koran and study Islam. (Frankly, I'm not sure who was happier when I was freed—they or I.)

From Captive to Convert

Back home in London, I kept my word about studying Islam—and was amazed by what I discovered. I'd been expecting Koran chapters on how to beat your wife and oppress your daughters; instead, I found passages promoting the liberation of women. Two-and-a-half years after my capture, I converted to Islam, provoking a mixture of astonishment, disappointment and encouragement among friends and relatives.

Now, it is with disgust and dismay that I watch here in Britain as former foreign secretary Jack Straw describes the Muslim nikab—a face veil that reveals only the eyes—as an unwelcome barrier to integration, with Prime Minister Tony Blair, writer Salman Rushdie and even Italian Prime Minister Romano Prodi leaping to his defense.

"Islam Offers Women So Much"

Having been on both sides of the veil, I can tell you that most Western male politicians and journalists who lament the oppression of women in the Islamic world have no idea what they are talking about. They go on about veils, child brides, female circumcision, honor killings and forced marriages, and they wrongly blame Islam for all this—their arrogance surpassed only by their ignorance.

These cultural issues and customs have nothing to do with Islam. A careful reading of the Koran shows that just about everything that Western feminists fought for in the 1970s was available to Muslim

Some argue that veiling helps Islamic women be respected for their mind and personality rather than their appearance.

women 1,400 years ago. Women in Islam are considered equal to men in spirituality, education and worth, and a woman's gift for childbirth and child-rearing is regarded as a positive attribute.

When Islam offers women so much, why are Western men so obsessed with Muslim women's attire? Even British government ministers Gordon Brown and John Reid have made disparaging remarks about the nikab—and they hail from across the Scottish border, where men wear skirts.

The Veil Offers Women Modesty and Pride

When I converted to Islam and began wearing a headscarf, the repercussions were enormous. All I did was cover my head and hair—but I instantly became a second-class citizen. I knew I'd hear from the odd Islamophobe, but I didn't expect so much open hostility from strangers. Cabs passed me by at night, their "for hire" lights glowing. One cabbie, after dropping off a white passenger right in front of me, glared at me when I rapped on his window, then drove off. Another said, "Don't leave a bomb in the back seat" and asked, "Where's bin Laden hiding?"

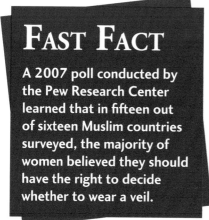

FAST FACT

A 2007 poll conducted by the Pew Research Center learned that in fifteen out of sixteen Muslim countries surveyed, the majority of women believed they should have the right to decide whether to wear a veil.

Yes, it is a religious obligation for Muslim women to dress modestly, but the majority of Muslim women I know like wearing the hijab, which leaves the face uncovered, though a few prefer the nikab. It is a personal statement: My dress tells you that I am a Muslim and that I expect to be treated respectfully, much as a Wall Street banker would say that a business suit defines him as an executive to be taken seriously. And, especially among converts to the faith like me, the attention of men who confront women with inappropriate, leering behavior is not tolerable.

The Veil Is a Symbol of Feminism

I was a Western feminist for many years, but I've discovered that Muslim feminists are more radical than their secular counterparts.

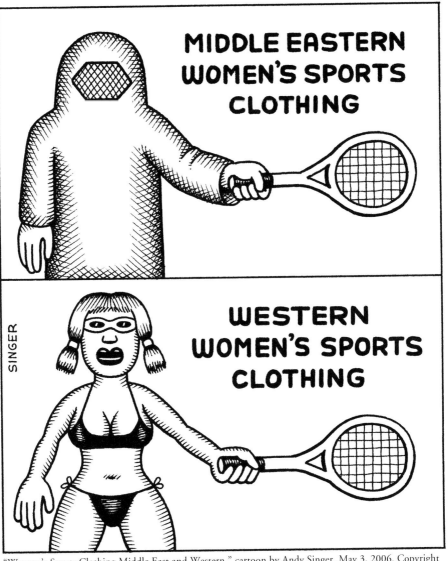

We hate those ghastly beauty pageants, and tried to stop laughing in 2003 when judges of the Miss Earth competition hailed the emergence of a bikini-clad Miss Afghanistan, Vida Samadzai, as a giant leap for women's liberation. They even gave Samadzai a special award for "representing the victory of women's rights."

Some young Muslim feminists consider the hijab and the nikab political symbols, too, a way of rejecting Western excesses such as binge drinking, casual sex and drug use. What is more liberating:

being judged on the length of your skirt and the size of your surgically enhanced breasts, or being judged on your character and intelligence? In Islam, superiority is achieved through piety—not beauty, wealth, power, position or sex.

I didn't know whether to scream or laugh when Italy's Prodi joined the debate [in 2006] by declaring that it is "common sense" not to wear the nikab because it makes social relations "more difficult." Nonsense. If this is the case, then why are cellphones, landlines, e-mail, text messaging and fax machines in daily use? And no one switches off the radio because they can't see the presenter's face.

The Veil Encourages Respect, Not Violence

Under Islam, I am respected. It tells me that I have a right to an education and that it is my duty to seek out knowledge, regardless of whether I am single or married. Nowhere in the framework of Islam are we told that women must wash, clean or cook for men. As for how Muslim men are allowed to beat their wives—it's simply not true. Critics of Islam will quote random Koranic verses or hadith [oral traditions], but usually out of context. If a man does raise a finger against his wife, he is not allowed to leave a mark on her body, which is the Koran's way of saying, "Don't beat your wife, stupid."

It is not just Muslim men who must reevaluate the place and treatment of women. According to a recent National Domestic Violence Hotline survey, 4 million American women experience a serious assault by a partner during an average 12-month period. More than three women are killed by their husbands and boyfriends every day—that is nearly 5,500 since 9/11.

Violent men don't come from any particular religious or cultural category; one in three women around the world has been beaten, coerced into sex or otherwise abused in her lifetime, according to the hotline survey. This is a global problem that transcends religion, wealth, class, race and culture.

Women Are Subjugated in the West More than in Islam

But it is also true that in the West, men still believe that they are superior to women, despite protests to the contrary. They still receive better pay for equal work—whether in the mailroom or the boardroom—and women are still treated as sexualized commodities whose power and influence flow directly from their appearance.

And for those who are still trying to claim that Islam oppresses women, recall this 1992 statement from the Rev. Pat Robertson, offering his views on empowered women: Feminism is a "socialist, anti-family political movement that encourages women to leave their husbands, kill their children, practice witchcraft, destroy capitalism and become lesbians."

Now you tell me who is civilized and who is not.

EVALUATING THE AUTHOR'S ARGUMENTS:

Yvonne Ridley converted to Islam after she was captured by the Taliban, the former rulers of Afghanistan. Does knowing the author's background influence your opinion of her argument? If so, in what way?

The Veil Violates Women's Rights

Danielle Crittenden

"*What the [Ku Klux] Klan outfit represents to someone of African-American descent is exactly what the burka should represent to every free woman.*"

Writer Danielle Crittenden conducted a social experiment in which she wore a burka, a head-to-toe veil popular in Saudi Arabia, around Washington, D.C., for several days. In the following viewpoint she explains why she thinks veils violate women's rights. Muslim societies use the veil to cover up women because men are unable to control their sexuality, she explains. Keeping them covered relegates them to second-class citizens, which in turn makes it easier for men to subjugate women in other ways, she says, such as oppressing, maiming, even murdering them. Crittenden concludes that the veil is a dangerous tool used by Muslim cultures to excuse violence against women. It prevents women from participating fully and equally in society, and thus Crittenden recommends it not be tolerated in free, Western societies.

Danielle Crittenden, "Islamic Like Me: Why the Veil Is a Threat," HuffingtonPost.com, December 13, 2007. Reproduced by permission.

My series about my adventures in a Saudi burka[1] generated a lot of fascinating comments [by readers] . . . who insisted that our Western culture was more sexually oppressive than the burka. Today I'll deal with the frequently-made-observation by readers: If a woman wants to wear a burka in a democratic society, what's it to us?

The Veil Is a Symbol of an Intolerant Culture

Just because veiling is culturally different from our customs, why should we feel threatened by it?

A good question. Tolerance of other cultures and religions is one of the founding pillars of a democratic society. Certainly I found the tolerance with which I was greeted all week in my burka to some degree heartening: Whatever thoughts, opinions, surprise, fear or anger my appearance provoked in others was, with rare exception, suppressed; everywhere I went most people went out of their way to be polite— when they weren't utterly indifferent to how I looked.

Yet tolerance in a free society should not extend to accepting (or ignoring) practices that violate our laws and our norms. Honor killings; female genital mutilation; female illiteracy; women forced to hide their faces in public; women forbidden to leave the house without the company of a man: these are phenomena which we, in the West, imagine happen in other places, to women far away in the Middle East or living among distant Muslim tribes.

But we are out of touch with what is happening in democratic societies—until it is shockingly brought to our attention. The

---

1. The author conducted a social experiment in which she walked around Washington, D.C., for several days in a burka.

In Britain, Muslim women are increasingly speaking out against Islamic laws that they say subjugate women.

murder of a 16-year-old Muslim girl by her father in Toronto—allegedly for the girl's refusal to wear hijab [a veil]—is now being decried as Canada's first honor killing. It may better be described as the first one we officially know about. For how many of us here know that female genital mutilation takes place in the United States? How many of us realize that women in allegedly free societies such as Holland and England are being imprisoned in their homes, by their own husbands and parents? How many are aware that women in places as familiar as northern Italy or upstate New York have been victims of the "honor killings?"

In Western democracies, religious freedom is not only tolerated but encouraged. Women's rights are not only respected, but legally enforced. Most of the time, these two principles are thoroughly compatible. Yet in recent years, women's rights have been systematically undermined by Islamic religious authorities operating in full and knowledgeable defiance of the law. . . .

The Veil Is Used to Imprison Women

Consider what is happening already. . . .

The BBC reported that a Muslim dentist in Bury, England made a woman wear Islamic dress as the price of accepting her as a patient in the National Health Service. The dentist is said to have told the patient that unless she wore a headscarf she would have to find another practice. . . .

In Derby, England, an 18-year-old woman named Lina finally escaped to a women's shelter after being imprisoned by her parents in their home. Until then, Lina had never worn Western clothing. Her parents, immigrants from Pakistan, insisted she wear the jilbab, a head-to-toe covering favored by conservative Muslims. When she turned 16, her parents informed her that she was "engaged" to her first cousin, a 21-year-old man she detested. When she balked, her parents withdrew her from school and locked her in her room, where they told her she would remain until she consented. They padlocked her door, locked the windows, installed spikes along the top of the backyard fence so she couldn't climb over. For two years, she was allowed out of her room only to do housework, and beaten frequently. . . .

The Veil Represents Heinous Crimes Against Women

The tribal practice of female circumcision/genital mutilation is being forced upon girls in the United States and other Western countries.

- From the *Boston Globe*: Based on the census data of 2000, the African Women's Health Center at Brigham & Women's Hospital, which tracks the practice, estimates that 228,000 girls and women in the United States have either undergone female genital mutilation or are at risk. "Some experts who work in the communities, say they have not seen evidence of a flourishing underground practice . . . [but] they do believe . . . that some immigrants might send their daughters back to their native countries for the procedure. . . ."
- From the same source above: In Seattle in 1996, Somali mothers giving birth at the Harborview Medical Center requested that their daughters be circumcised [mutilated] as well as their sons. The hospital devised a compromise: the girls would be "nicked" on the clitoral hood, in a symbolic gesture meant to deter the

families from performing the traditional practice. The plan, which the immigrants supported, was to perform the procedure under local anesthetic when the girls were old enough to give informed consent. When news of the proposal broke, public outrage forced the hospital to back down from its compromise.

Women are being murdered on Western soil, victims of "honor killings."

- In 2004, a Turkish immigrant was charged with killing his wife and critically injuring his two daughters in their Scottsville, NY townhouse. In his court defense, he argued that he had acted as a matter of honor: He had attacked his wife and daughters after learning that his brother had molested them. He also said his four-year-old daughter had been "sullied" by a gynecological exam. . . .

Veils Are Used to Control Women

And these are only a handful of examples that have taken place worldwide in democratic countries. So to go back to my original question: What does all this have to do with tolerating a woman on the subway with a burka?

I would argue: Everything. The more pervasive and familiar a sight it becomes in our society, the more indifferent we will become to its meaning—and to those who are forced to wear it. For the burka . . . is not itself a religious garment: "North American and European Muslim leaders insist that the Koran does not require full cover-up, that little more is required than modest clothes and a headscarf." Indeed, there is much debate within Muslim circles as to what the few vague verses in the Koran that refer to female dress actually mean (just Google "hijab" and you'll pull up dozens of sites engaged in this very question). What it is is a cultural and even political garment, imposed upon women in societies where they are regarded as property, not human beings. Even if a woman takes it up willingly—as some do—that doesn't detract from the burka's symbolism. As some [readers] have noted, many of these women veil themselves in order to protest Western culture and show their defiance towards it.

That's honest of them—and we should be honest in return, by not accepting their defiance—nor their forced compliance—in our free societies. . . . I [have] compared the wearing of a burka with the wearing of a [Ku Klux] Klan robe:

If I had chosen to walk about Washington in a white hood and sheets rather than black ones, I doubt I would have encountered such universal politeness. And yet, what the Klan outfit represents to someone of African-American descent is exactly what the burka should represent to every free woman. Those who impose it upon women believe that a whole category of human beings can be treated as property; that this category may be beaten, sold into marriage, divorced at whim, denied education and work, raped with impunity, and stoned to death for offenses that would be

pardoned in a man. For the wearer of the white hood, the subjugated category is defined by race. For the wearer of the black hood, it's defined by sex. Otherwise the two garments carry the same meaning—with the slight variation that one is worn by the would-be oppressor, the other by the oppressed.

The Veil Is a Violation of Human Rights

For this reason, and as the price of joining secular society, the French and Turkish governments have taken steps to ban all forms of hijab. Americans needn't—and obviously shouldn't—have to go that far. Minimally, we should not cave to pressure tactics nor tolerate customs that are hostile to a democratic understanding of human rights.

Many societies have recognized that under certain circumstances, concealment is something more than a personal choice. As long ago as 1875, the U.S. Congress attempted to prohibit the wearing of Ku Klux Klan robes. In the last days before the fascist takeover, the Italian parliament banned the face masks worn by fascist bands. Kemal Ataturk's Turkish reformers banned hijab—not only the veil, but even just the head covering—in all public places.

I'm hanging up my burka for now. It's lovely to breathe in fresh air again—both literally, without a mask, and figuratively, in the debate my series has inspired among you. That's what we do in a free society—debate, women equally alongside men.

EVALUATING THE AUTHORS' ARGUMENTS:

In this viewpoint, Danielle Crittenden compares the veil to the white robes adopted by the racist group the Ku Klux Klan. In the previous viewpoint Yvonne Ridley compares the veil to a business suit. What does each author mean by their comparisons? Which outfit do you think the veil more closely resembles—a Klan robe or a business suit? Explain your reasoning.

Islam Condemns Honor Killings

Melissa Robinson

"The problem of domestic violence is not unique to Muslims."

In the following viewpoint, Melissa Robinson argues that nowhere in Islam are honor killings encouraged or condoned. Rather, the Koran states that women and girls are supposed to be honored by their families and never abused, hurt, or murdered. Robinson acknowledges that honor killings are a problem in Muslim societies, but she points out that there are many cultures and religions that experience domestic violence and murder. She explains that misogynistic (anti-woman) statements have been made not just by Muslim imams (religious leaders) but also by Christian saints, Italian philosophers, American revolutionaries, French existentialists, Baptist preachers, historians, scientists, poets, and others. She concludes that honor killings are not inherently an Islamic problem; however, when they occur in Muslim families, they should be condemned by Muslims everywhere as being un-Islamic.

Melissa Robinson is the director and cofounder of the American Islamic Fellowship.

AS YOU READ, CONSIDER THE FOLLOWING QUESTIONS:
1. Who is Sandela Kanwal?
2. What two verses does the author quote from the Koran? How do these help support her argument?
3. What is Baitul Salaam, as described by the author?

As an American Muslim, I was horrified to read about the tragic death of Sandela Kanwal in Clayton County, Ga., allegedly at the hands of her father in a supposed "honor killing."

According to area police, Kanwal's father killed her because she left her husband. According to the twisted logic of "honor killings," Kanwal ruined the "honor" of the family by leaving her arranged marriage.

Islam Never Allows Murder

It would be easy to point a finger at all Muslims and rail against such barbaric traditions. But this I can tell you: I am a Muslim, born and raised in Tennessee, and I do not subscribe to this brand of honor.

As a co-founder of the American Islamic Fellowship, an Atlanta area organization of more than 200 Muslims, I can tell you that our organization does not subscribe to any interpretation of Islam that condones murder in the name of religion or honor. To me and our membership, this is an abhorrent expression of a universal phenomenon of misogynistic thinking that targets women as the guardians of a community's honor.

All Cultures Struggle with Domestic Violence

It comes from the mouths of Christian saints, Italian philosophers, American revolutionaries, French existentialists, Baptist preachers, modern historians, European scientists, English poets, and Muslim imams, just to name a few: "It is still Eve the temptress that we must beware of in every woman." "It is said in the state of adultery, the responsibility falls 90 per cent of the time on the woman." Why?

"Because she possesses the weapon of enticement," and "A wife is to submit herself graciously to the servant leadership of her husband."

Honor Killings in America

Honor killings happen all over the world, even in the United States.

Victim Name (age)	Year, Location	Reason	Method
Palestina Isa (16)	1989 St. Louis, MO	"too American," refused to travel with her father	stabbed thirteen times by father as her mother held her down
Methal Deyam (22)	1999 Cleveland, OH	refused to marry her cousin; attended college	two cousins allegedly shot her; choked on own blood
Lubaina Bhatti Ahmed (39)	1999 St. Clairsville, OH	filed for divorce	throat cut; her father's sister and niece's throats were also cut
Farah Kahn (5)	1999 Toronto, Canada	was suspected of carrying a stranger's child	father and stepmother cut her throat; dismembered her body
Shahpara Sayeed (33)	2000 Chicago, IL	motive is unclear	burned alive
Marlyn Hassan (29)	2002 Jersey City, NJ	refused to convert from Hinduism to Islam	husband, an auto mechanic, stabbed wife (and the twins in her womb), the wife's sister, and the wife's mother
Hatice Peltek (39)	2004 Scottsville, NY	had been molested by brother-in-law	stabbed, bludgeoned with hammer along with daughters
Amina Said (17)	2008 Irving, TX	had "Western" ways	shot
Sarah Said (18)	2008 Irving, TX	had "Western" ways	shot
Fauzia Mohammed (19)	2008 Henrietta, NY	too "Western," immodest clothing, planned to attend college in New York City	stabbed
Sandeela Kanwal (25)	2008 Atlanta, GA	filed for divorce after arranged marriage	strangled

Taken from: Phyllis Chesler, "Are Honor Killings Simply Domestic Violence?" *Middle East Quarterly*, Spring 2009.

Who said which comment? The first came from St. Augustine, the second from an Imam in Australia, and the third from a Baptist preacher.

While the problem of domestic violence is not unique to Muslims, we are still struggling to eliminate this kind of "honor killing" from our communities internationally. In Pakistan, a predominantly Muslim country, there were 107 honor crimes [in 2007], according to the Pakistan Human Rights Commission. It is critical that we speak out.

The Qur'an Condemns Violence Against Family

The Qur'an states, "Show kindness to parents, and to family, and orphans, and the needy, and to the neighbour who is of your kin and the neighbour who is not of kin, and the fellow-traveller and the wayfarer" and "When you divorce wives, and they are about to reach their term, then hold them back honorably or set them free honorably; and hold them not back by injuring them so that you commit aggression, and whoever commits that, then indeed he does wrong." This means that we cannot, under any circumstances, allow physical abuse in families. To do so would be to violate these fundamental Qur'anic injunctions.

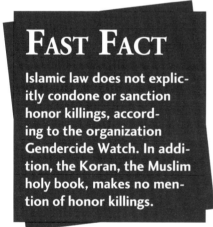

FAST FACT

Islamic law does not explicitly condone or sanction honor killings, according to the organization Gendercide Watch. In addition, the Koran, the Muslim holy book, makes no mention of honor killings.

I call upon all Muslim leaders and mosques to preach from the pulpit this Friday [the Muslim holy day] that this kind of violence is unacceptable. We need to help our communities heal and lead the way to a brighter, safer future. We need to stop allowing our religious texts to be used to justify cruel behavior. We have a humanitarian obligation to speak out against those who commit such atrocities.

Muslims Must Speak Out Against Violence Done in Islam's Name

As a Muslim, I have a religious obligation to speak out against oppression and injustice and to protect the rights of the disenfranchised. As

In India Muslim men warily watch Muslim women protest an honor killing. The author states the Koran says women and girls are to be honored by their families, not abused.

a woman and a Muslim I am horrified by the tragedy of Sandela's death; I refuse to allow her death to be swept under the rug.

I invite all people of faith to join me in denouncing all kinds of violence and abuse. We must work together to bring an end to this malady that afflicts us all.

In Atlanta, the organizations dedicated to fighting domestic violence are always in need of our support.

A few of these in the Atlanta area include the Muslim-run women's shelter, Baitul Salaam, the South Asian organization, Raksha, in addition to the Women's Resource Center for Domestic Violence, the Partnership Against Domestic Violence, and the International Women's House.

Last March [2008], the American Islamic Fellowship in partnership with the Progressive Muslim Network in Washington D.C. and I AM: American Muslim in Phoenix, AZ launched "Not in Our Name: United Against Domestic Violence"—a campaign to unite all people of faith in an effort to bring an end to this problem that affects all of our communities. Another Muslim initiative to fight domestic violence internationally is the Peaceful Families Project.

We need to support these efforts so that no life is ever taken in the name of religion.

EVALUATING THE AUTHORS' ARGUMENTS:

Melissa Robinson casts the problem of honor killings as one of domestic violence. How do you think Robert Spencer, author of the next viewpoint, would respond to this characterization? Quote both authors in your answer.

Islam Condones Honor Killings

Robert Spencer

"Honor killing, the practice of murdering a female family member who is believed to have sullied the family honor, enjoys widespread acceptance in some areas of the Islamic world."

In the following viewpoint Robert Spencer argues that Islam is used to justify honor killings, which are the murder of girls and women who have betrayed their family's honor. He discusses the case of two teen-age Muslims who were killed by their father because they had boyfriends. Spencer says that although there is nothing in the Koran, the Muslim holy book, that encourages men to kill women for such an offense, such crimes occur too often in Muslim societies and families to simply be a matter of domestic violence. Furthermore, he cites examples of Muslim countries in which Islam has been used to justify violence against women. Spencer says that it is impossible to claim that Islam has nothing to do with honor killings when the majority of such murders occur in Islamic contexts. Spencer encourages Muslim leaders around the world to speak out about this injustice if they truly believe their religion has nothing to do with it.

Robert Spencer, "Honor Killing in Texas," *Human Events*, vol. 64, January 14, 2008. Copyright © 2008 Human Events Inc. Reproduced by permission.

Robert Spencer is the director of Jihad Watch, an organization that keeps tabs on Islamic extremism. He is the author of *The Politically Incorrect Guide to Islam (and the Crusades)* and *The Truth About Muhammad.*

AS YOU READ, CONSIDER THE FOLLOWING QUESTIONS:
1. Who is Yaser Abdel Said?
2. Who is Aqsa Parvez?
3. On what grounds did the Jordanian parliament vote against increasing penalties for honor killings in 2003?

Amina Said, 18, and her sister Sarah, 17, smile happily in one widely circulating photo, and Amina is wearing what looks like a sweatshirt bearing the name "AMERICA." But their fate may have been the herald of a new, disquieting feature of the American landscape: honor killing. Amina and Sarah were shot dead in Irving, Texas, on New Year's Day. Police are searching for their father, Yaser Abdel Said, on a warrant for capital murder.

An Honor Killing in Texas

The girls' great aunt, Gail Gartrell, told reporters, "This was an honor killing." She explained that Yaser Said had long abused the girls, and after discovering that they had boyfriends, had threatened to kill them—whereupon their mother fled with them. "She ran with them," said Gartrell, "because she knew he would carry out the threat." But Said found them, and apparently did carry it out.

Honor killing, the practice of murdering a female family member who is believed to have sullied the family honor, enjoys widespread acceptance in some areas of the Islamic world. However, Islam Said, the brother of Amina and Sarah, has denied that the murders had anything to do with Islam at all. "It's not religion," he insisted. "It's something else. Religion has nothing to do with it."

And to be sure, the Qur'an or Islamic tradition does not sanction honor killing. Muslim spokesmen have hastened, after the recent killing in Canada of another teenage Muslim girl, Aqsa Parvez, by her father to tell the public that honor killing has nothing to do with

Islam, but is merely a feature of Islamic Culture in some areas. Aqsa Parvez was sixteen years old; her father, Muhammad Parvez, has been charged with strangling her to death because she refused to wear the hijab. Shahina Siddiqui, president of the Islamic Social Services Association, declared: "The strangulation death of Ms. Parvez was the result of domestic violence, a problem that cuts across Canadian society and is blind to colour or creed." Sheikh Alaa El-Sayyed, imam of the Islamic Society of North America in Mississauga, Ontario, agreed: "The bottom line is, it's a domestic violence issue."

Islam Has Been Used to Justify Honor Killings
But these dismissals are too easy, principally because they fail to take into account important evidence. In some areas, honor killing is assumed to

Mourners in Mississauga, Ontario, Canada, attend a memorial service for honor killing victim Aqsa Parvez. She was murdered by her father for refusing to wear the hijab.

Honor Killings Versus Domestic Violence

Some cast honor killings as a form of domestic violence, but there are distinct differences.

Honor Killings	Domestic Violence
Committed mainly by Muslims against Muslim girls/young adult women.	Committed by men of all faiths usually against adult women.
Committed mainly by fathers against their teenage daughters and daughters in their early twenties. Wives and older-age daughters may also be victims, but to a lesser extent.	Committed by an adult male spouse against an adult female spouse or intimate partner.
Carefully planned. Death threats are often used as a means of control.	The murder is often unplanned and spontaneous.
The planning and execution involve multiple family members and can include mothers, sisters, brothers, male cousins, uncles, grandfathers, etc. If the girl escapes, the extended family will continue to search for her to kill her.	The murder is carried out by one man with no family complicity.
The reason given for the honor killing is that the girl or young woman has "dishonored" the family.	The batterer-murderer does not claim any family concept of "honor." The reasons may range from a poorly cooked meal to suspected infidelity to the woman's trying to protect the children from his abuse or turning to the authorities for help.
At least half the time, the killings are carried out with barbaric ferocity. The female victim is often raped, burned alive, stoned or beaten to death, cut at the throat, decapitated, stabbed numerous times, suffocated slowly, etc.	While some men do beat a spouse to death, they often simply shoot or stab them.
The extended family and community valorize the honor killing. They do not condemn the perpetrators in the name of Islam. Mainly, honor killings are seen as normative.	The batterer-murderer is seen as a criminal; no one defends him as a hero. Such men are often viewed as sociopaths, mentally ill, or evil.

Taken from: Phyllis Chesler, "Are Honor Killings Simply Domestic Violence?" *Middle East Quarterly*, Spring 2009, pp. 61–69.

be an Islamic practice. There is evidence that Islamic culture inculcates [teaches by frequent instruction] attitudes that could lead directly to the murders of these two girls in Texas. In 2003, the Jordanian Parliament voted down on Islamic grounds a provision designed to stiffen penalties for honor killings. In a sadly typical consequence of this, a Jordanian man who murdered his sister because he thought she had a lover was given a three-month sentence, which was suspended for time served, allowing him to walk free. The *Yemen Times* published an article insisting that violence against women is necessary for the stability of the family and the society, and invoking Islam to support this view.

Since Islam is used as the justification for such barbarities, it becomes incumbent upon

Muslim spokesmen to confront this directly, and to work for positive change, rather than simply to consign it all to culture, as if that absolves Islam from all responsibility. For this is the culture that apparently gave Yaser Said and Muhammad Parvez the idea that they had to kill their daughters. It is a culture suffused with its religion, thoroughly dominated by it—such that a clear distinction between the two is not so easy to find.

Muslim Leaders Must Speak Out

The killings of Amina and Sarah Said raises uncomfortable questions for the Islamic community in the United States, questions about the culture and mindset that people like Yaser Said bring to this country. Now that honor killing has come to Texas, Muslim spokesmen in the U.S. have an all the more urgent responsibility to end their denial and confront these cultural attitudes. If they don't, and instead continue to glibly insist that religion has nothing to do with what happened to these poor girls, the murders of the Said sisters will only be the beginning of a new American phenomenon.

EVALUATING THE AUTHORS' ARGUMENTS:

Spencer argues that Islam cannot be separated from honor killings because such murders occur so often in Muslim societies. How do you think Melissa Robinson, author of the previous viewpoint, would react to this reasoning? To what extent do you think honor killings are based in Islam? Explain your answer using evidence from the viewpoints you have read.

Chapter 3

What Reproductive Rights Should Women Have?

Forty years after the Supreme Court's controversial ruling on Roe v. Wade *women's reproductive rights are still a hot-button issue.*

Abortion Is a Woman's Right

Ann Furedi

"Abortion is a necessary back-up to birth control for any society that is committed to equality of opportunity for women."

In the following viewpoint Ann Furedi explains why it is a woman's right to access abortion. She explains that women must have complete control over their bodies in order to participate equally in society. Both men and women have sex, but Furedi points out that women are unique in that they alone must bear the consequences if that sex results in an unintended pregnancy. She says that abortion helps women be unfettered by this burden—it offers them autonomy over their bodies, which has been declared by the international community to be a key human right. This right is even more important when a pregnancy is caused by a rape or another unwanted sexual advance. Furedi concludes that no woman wants to need abortion, but keeping the procedure available and accessible is key to women's health and equality in society.

Ann Furedi is the chief executive of the British Pregnancy Advisory Service.

1. How many women in the United Kingdom does Furedi say can expect to have an abortion at some point in their lives?
2. According to Furedi, women need control over what in order to play an equal role in public life?
3. According to Furedi, what kind of issue has abortion been framed as since it was legalized in the United Kingdom in 1960?

'It is a common misperception that British law allows abortion on demand,' wrote *Times* science editor Mark Henderson on 28 November [2006], before explaining that women seeking an abortion 'must first jump through several medical and legal hoops'—including obtaining the approval of two doctors, who must justify their decisions on medical grounds. The two-doctor rule, he argued, 'does little but waste medical time and resources', and makes the abortion procedure more stressful for women than it needs to be: 'Some women . . . find it humiliating, to be declared at psychological risk when making a choice to end a pregnancy.'

Women Need to Be Able to Access Abortion

Henderson was responding to a major poll about attitudes to abortion in the UK, conducted by Ipsos Mori on behalf of bpas [British Pregnancy Advisory Service]. This follows two previous polls, in 1997 and 2001, and gives some important insights into the British public's views about abortion and how these have changed. So in 2006, it emerges that 63% of adults in the UK agreed that 'if a woman wants an abortion, she should not have to continue with her pregnancy', while only 18% disagreed. Furthermore, 59% agreed that 'abortion should be made legally available for all who want it'. This would require a change to the existing law, which requires two doctors to confirm that a woman meets certain criteria. Indeed, a change to this frankly arcane law, which as Henderson suggests serves no medical purpose, is long overdue.

Forty years on from the 1967 Abortion Act, the reality of abortion in the UK is very different. The abortion rate in 2005 was 17.8

Americans consistently support a woman's right to have an abortion in at least most cases.

"Do you think abortion should be legal in all cases, legal in most cases, illegal in most cases, or illegal in all cases?"

Year	Legal in All Cases	Legal in Most Cases	Illegal in Most Cases	Illegal in All Cases	Unsure
2008	22%	32%	26%	18%	3%
2007	20%	35%	25%	18%	2%
2005	17%	40%	27%	13%	3%
2004	21%	34%	25%	17%	3%
2003	23%	34%	25%	17%	2%
2001	22%	27%	28%	20%	3%

Taken from: ABC News/*Washington Post* poll, August 19–22, 2008.

per 1000 women aged 15–44, compared with 8 per 1000 women in 1970. At least one in three women in the UK can expect to have an abortion. Major advances have also been made in the provision and procedure of abortion: in particular, the development of Early Medical Abortion (the 'abortion pill') which provides a low-risk and easily administered form of termination of early pregnancy. It is now accepted that abortion is a fact of life: a necessary back-up to birth control for couples who want to plan their families. No woman ever wants to need to have an abortion, but those who do not want it to be legal are in a minority.

Abortion Is Too Tightly Regulated

Despite the mainstreaming of abortion in practice, however, the law on abortion remains restrictive. Britain is one of the few countries in Europe and North America that does not allow abortion on the woman's request at any stage. Abortion is our most tightly-regulated medical procedure, despite being shown to be a safe solution to a problem pregnancy. And yet, pro-choice advocates in Britain often seem wary of leading a discussion about reforming the abortion law, on the pragmatic grounds that the current legal framework allows women to access abortion on demand, even if it does not give them that right. Is that enough?

Abortion Is a Woman's Right

It seems unfashionably fundamentalist to defend the notion that women should have a 'right' to abortion. But we should remember what the concept of a right really means. The right to abortion and contraception was a basic tenet of the Women's Liberation Movement in its early years, along with the right to equal pay and equal job opportunities, because activists understood that women needed control over their fertility to play an equal role in public life. When you deny me a means to end my unwanted pregnancy, you deny me the opportunity to participate in society in the way that my brother or husband can. Better nurseries, better financial support can mitigate some of the consequences of motherhood—but nothing can mitigate the impact of pregnancy itself, which is why women need the means to end it.

This has not changed: it is as true in 2007 as it was in 1967. Contraception has improved, but is still fallible. Abortion is a necessary back-up to birth control for any society that is committed to equality of opportunity for women. The discourse of women's equality may have changed, but its fundamental prerequisites have not.

The Right to Bodily Autonomy

There is also another way in which the right to abortion must be nonnegotiable. When we are denied the right to end pregnancy we lose our right to bodily autonomy; a fundamental human right central to Western civilisation. The ethics of modern medical practice is built on the notion that each of us has the right to refuse to compromise our bodily integrity. You might find it morally reprehensible for me to refuse to give up a kidney that could be transplanted to save the life of my son, but there is no law to force me to do it. In the UK, the same is true of birth decisions. In refusing a Caesarean section delivery, I may condemn my unborn baby to certain death, but I commit no crime in doing so. No doctor can force me to accept a medical intervention against my consent, unless I am mentally incompetent.

The law forces us to draw a distinction between what is legal, and what we regard as morally right and wrong. We accept this because we accept that a society able to compel medical intervention without consent in the interests of someone else is a greater social evil than an occasional un-palatable individual choice. So it is interesting, for example, that in a question about approval of abortion in different circumstances, the recent Ipsos Mori poll found that less than half of the respondents—48%—said that they did not approve of abortion when the woman does not wish to have a child. But despite the fact they might not approve of abortion under particular circumstances, people thought women should be able to exercise that choice: with 63% agreeing that if a woman wants an abortion, she should not have to continue with her pregnancy.

Women Must Be Allowed to Make Their Own Choices

This unfashionable privileging of 'rights' is not divorced from the more acceptable stress on responsibility. Surely it is right, if not 'a right', for women to be allowed to make their own moral choices concerning their pregnancy. The decision must be made by someone: why should it not be made by the person whose life is most connected to it? In *Life's Dominion: An argument about abortion and euthanasia*, Ronald Dworkin argues compellingly that part of our belief in human dignity rests on people having 'the moral right and moral responsibility to confront the most fundamental questions about the meaning and value of their own lives for themselves.'

Each of us must be answerable to own conscience and conviction; this, he argues, is part of what makes us human. To take away our responsibility for our moral decisions is to take away our humanity. This argument implies we must allow people to make decisions that we believe are wrong—because it would be more wrong for us to deny them the capacity to do that. As Dworkin argues eloquently: 'Tolerance is the cost we must pay for our adventure in liberty'.

A Public Health Concern

Of course, we can be pragmatic—we don't have to talk in the language of rights. The UK provides an interesting example of where abortion access has been expanded and improved by a political administration that situates abortion, not as a right, but a public health concern. In the UK, the abortion discourse has been almost silent as to 'rights'. Since abortion was legalised in the 1960s, it has been treated as a matter of public health. The framing of abortion in a personal and public health context has made it difficult to oppose. When abortion is seen as a health matter, to argue against abortion is to argue against a doctor's decision of what is best for a patient.

The public health arguments for abortion have potential to unite social liberals and conservatives. Even those who think abortion is abhorrent draw back from the practical consequences of making it unlawful. In the UK there is a broad consensus that abortion is a 'lesser evil', a wrong that is sometimes right.

> **FAST FACT**
>
> According to a British pro-choice organization, more than 66,000 women die each year because they are unable to access safe, legal abortion services; more than 5 million are hospitalized because of complications from unsafe abortions.

It may be that the arguments around public health are where we can establish the greatest consensus on abortion's acceptability. However, any such consensus will be partial because the moral dimension will remain contentious. This is inevitable and insurmountable. There can be no moral consensus that includes those who believe that the destruction of human life in the womb is wrong and those who believe it is not. It may be possible to establish a pragmatic consensus among those who are prepared to discuss which abortions are less wrong than others, but attempts to establish foundations for a broader moral consensus degenerate into glibness.

Resolving the Morality of Abortion

Witness, for example, the extent to which many opponents of abortion in the UK now focus their arguments on the problem of late

Pro-life and pro-choice supporters confront each other in London over whether the legal limit for abortion should be twenty-four weeks of pregnancy or less.

abortions, using emotive images of walking and smiling fetuses and contested claims about fetal pain. Rather than arguing whether abortion is right or wrong, the legal debate tends to become focused around the 24-week 'time limit', and debates about fetal development push the principled issue of women's rights into the background. This is not a debate we can shy away from—and nor should we want to.

The morality of abortion cannot be resolved in the abstract. Each individual abortion takes place within its own complex set of circumstances. To understand abortion we need to understand its place [in] women's lives. From the findings of the Ipsos Mori poll, public opinion seems to be more progressive than politicians think. It may be that we can best build support for legal abortion by putting the spin to one side and telling the whole truth: the truth about what abortion is, the truth about why women have them, and the truth about what it means for women when bodily autonomy is denied.

To defend abortion we must win arguments in favour of tolerance and encourage an aspiration for liberty. To win the arguments, first we must have them.

EVALUATING THE AUTHOR'S ARGUMENTS:

Ann Furedi argues that having access to abortion offers a woman the opportunity to participate in society the way her brother and husband can. In five to six sentences, clarify what she means by this. Do you think she is right? Explain your answer thoroughly.

Viewpoint

2

Abortion Is Not a Woman's Right

Randy Alcorn

"There can be no equal rights for all women until there are equal rights for unborn women."

In the following viewpoint (excerpted from an online article, see citation), Randy Alcorn argues that abortion is not a women's rights issue. Alcorn rejects the suggestion that women have any rights to gain from abortion. Rather, he contends that when women access abortion, they violate their own right to happiness. Furthermore, in Alcorn's opinion, one can be a feminist without supporting abortion. He points out that Susan B. Anthony never saw abortion as a women's rights issue—yet no one would deny she was one of America's founding feminists. Alcorn says that many women have been tricked into thinking that abortion is a woman's right by men who seek to abdicate their responsibility as fathers. He concludes there will never be equal rights for all women unless there are equal rights for unborn women.

Randy Alcorn is the founder and director of Eternal Perspective Ministries, a non-profit organization dedicated to teaching biblical principles and drawing attention to the needy.

Randy Alcorn, "Is Abortion Really a Women's Rights Issue?" Eternal Perspective Ministries, 2008. www.epm.org/artman2/publish/Prolife_abortion/Is_Abortion_Really_a_Women_s_Rights_Issue.shtml. Reproduced by permission.

AS YOU READ, CONSIDER THE FOLLOWING QUESTIONS:
1. Who does Alcorn say referred to abortion as "child murder"?
2. What is "terrorist feminism," as described by one feminist?
3. According to the author, how many fetuses in Bombay, India, were aborted after mothers learned they were carrying girls?

Kate Michelman, former president of NARAL [a pro-choice organization], says: "We have to remind people that abortion is the guarantor of a woman's . . . right to participate fully in the social and political life of society." But a pregnant woman *can* fully participate in society. And if she can't, isn't the solution changing society rather than killing children?

Women Do Not Gain Rights by Killing Their Children

"How can women achieve equality without control of their reproductive lives?" Feminists for Life responds:

> The premise of the question is the premise of male domination throughout the millennia—that it was nature which made men superior and women inferior. Medical technology is offered as a solution to achieve equality; but the premise is wrong. . . . It's an insult to women to say women must change their biology in order to fit into society.

In her essay, "Feminism: Bewitched by Abortion," environmentalist Rosemary Bottcher argues that the feminist movement has degraded women by portraying them as unable to handle the stress and pressures of pregnancy without resorting to killing their children.

Abortion Is Not Just Surgery

Pro-choice groups consistently oppose efforts to require that abortion be treated like every other surgery when it comes to informing the patient of its nature and risks. They don't seem to believe that women are capable of making intelligent choices after being presented with the facts.

Early suffragette Alice Paul, who drafted the original Equal Rights Amendment, argued that abortion was "the ultimate exploitation of women."

Serrin Foster, president of Feminists for Life, speaks powerfully in "The Feminist Case Against Abortion." She says that historically the primary activists against abortion were women, and ironically "the anti-abortion laws that early feminists worked so hard to enact to protect women and children were the very ones destroyed by the *Roe v. Wade* decision 100 years later."

Many Feminists Have Been Against Abortion

Susan B. Anthony stood for women's rights at a time when women weren't even allowed to vote. She referred to abortion as "child murder" and viewed it as a means of exploiting both women and children. Anthony wrote, "I deplore the horrible crime of child murder. . . . No matter what the motive, love of ease, or a desire to save from suffering the unborn innocent, the woman is awfully guilty who commits the deed."

Anthony's newspaper, *The Revolution*, made this claim: "When a woman destroys the life of her unborn child, it is a sign that, by education or circumstances, she has been greatly wronged."

Anthony and other feminists who opposed abortion were followed decades later by a new breed of feminists. Most prominent was Margaret Sanger, who advocated abortion as a means of eugenics, economics, and sexual liberation. After eugenics fell into disfavor following the Holocaust, her organization went underground, then later resurfaced as the Planned Parenthood Federation. Sanger and others who followed Anthony tried to tie the abortion agenda to the legitimate issues of women's rights.

Dr. Bernard Nathanson says that in the 1960s, he and his fellow abortion-rights strategists deliberately linked abortion to the women's issue so it could be furthered not on its own merits but on the merits of women's rights. Abortion rode on the coattails of women's rights.

Alice Paul drafted the original version of the Equal Rights Amendment (ERA), a landmark feminist document. But Alice Paul referred to abortion as "the ultimate exploitation of women."

One feminist has labeled the attempt to marry feminism to abortion as "terrorist feminism." In her words, it forces the feminist to be "willing to kill for the cause you believe in." In their publication *The American Feminist*, Feminists for Life features the beautiful face of a child and asks, "Is this the face of the enemy?" They argue

> ## FAST FACT
>
> As of May 2007, there were laws in twenty-five states that said if a pregnant woman is murdered, her unborn embryo or fetus can also be counted as a victim of homicide.

"Life-ectomy," cartoon by Gary McCoy, Cagle Cartoons, April 24, 2007. Copyright © 2007 by Gary McCoy, CagleCartoons.com and PoliticalCartoons.com. All rights reserved.

that they stand on two hundred years of pro-life feminist history, and that it wasn't until the 1970s that the women's movement embraced abortion.

Abortion Favors Men, Not Women

Polls indicate that more women than men affirm the unborns' right to life. In fact, "the most pro-abortion category in the United States (and also in other nations) is white males between the ages of twenty and forty-five. More specifically, "the group that is most consistently pro-choice is actually single men." It's ironic that abortion has been turned into a women's rights issue when it has encouraged male irresponsibility and failure to care for women and children. Shouldn't men be called upon to do more than just provide money to kill a child? Shouldn't they be encouraged instead to say to the woman they've made pregnant, "I'll be there for our child. I'll do everything I can for her. And if you're willing to have me, I'll be there for you too."

Abortion Is Being Used to Eliminate Women

One of the ironies of feminism is that by its advocacy of abortion it has endorsed the single greatest means of robbing women of their most basic right—the right to life.

Abortion has become the primary means of eliminating unwanted females across the globe. A survey of a dozen villages in India uncovered a frightening statistic: out of a total population of ten thousand, only fifty were girls. The other girls, thousands of them, had been killed by abortion. In Bombay, of eight thousand amniocentesis tests indicating the babies were female, all but one of the girls were killed by abortion.

Because of sex-selection abortions, two-thirds of children born in China are now males. In the countryside, the ratio of boys to girls is four to one.

Amniocentesis is also being used to detect a child's gender in America. *Medical World News* reported a study in which ninety-nine mothers were informed of the sex of their children. Fifty-three of these preborns were boys and forty-six were girls. Only one mother elected to abort her boy, while twenty-nine elected to abort their girls.

More girls than boys are now being killed by abortion. To kill an unborn female is to kill a young woman. There can be no equal rights for all women until there are equal rights for unborn women.

(Footnotes from this edited article may be found in chapter 8 of *Why ProLife?* by Randy Alcorn [Sisters, OR: Multnomah Publishers, 2004].)

EVALUATING THE AUTHOR'S ARGUMENTS:

Alcorn argues that abortion violates women's rights. How do you think each of the other authors in this chapter might respond to this suggestion? List each author and write two to three sentences on what you think their response might be. Then, state your position on the matter—do you think having access to abortion improves women's rights or violates them?

Women Should Have to Consider Men's Feelings When Considering Abortion

Courtney E. Martin

"There must be a way to talk about men's perspectives and experiences without compromising women's bodies."

Courtney E. Martin is the author of *Perfect Girls, Starving Daughters: The Frightening New Normalcy of Hating Your Body*. In the following viewpoint she argues that it is important that both men's and women's feelings be considered when an abortion occurs. Too often, says Martin, men are pushed outside of the abortion discussion because it is considered a woman's issue. Although she acknowledges that men should not be able to tell women whether or not to have an abortion, their feelings on the matter deserve to be heard. Letting men voice their feelings on abortion helps them deal with this important event, and it also prevents women from bearing the burden of the decision alone. Both men and women have a lot to gain by incorporating men's feelings into the abortion discussion, concludes Martin.

AS YOU READ, CONSIDER THE FOLLOWING QUESTIONS:
1. Who is Cody, and how does he factor into the author's argument?
2. Who are too often thought of as "coat holders and drivers," in Shostak's opinion? What does she mean by this?
3. In Martin's opinion, what can keep abortion safe and less stigmatized for everyone?

When I was in high school, one of my friends got a secret abortion. Though I wasn't raised in a religious household, I remember taking a sheet of white, clean paper and writing a series of haphazard prayers that I then hid in my sock drawer.

One of them was for Cody,* my friend's bewildered boyfriend. She wanted nothing to do with him, though he was trying his 17-year-old-teenage-boy best to be supportive; she said it felt like Cody had done this *to* her. I understood, but I also knew that he must be—as she was—holding it together all day, crying alone at night, utterly confused. Though raised Catholic, he too thought an abortion was the right decision, but had no role in the ritual of that choice.

I think of Cody from time to time and wonder what he's doing now. I recently heard a rumor that he's gone on to study theology. I can't help but wonder if that decision was in some way informed by the conversation he was never able to have—with her, with friends, with mentors, with his version of god—about his experience of abortion.

After all, where is a pro-choice man who wants guidance, community or counseling around his experience of abortion to turn?

Men Are Affected by Abortion, Too

In the public sphere, the most vocal mention of men and abortion comes in virulently unsympathetic forms: government officials' ethically indefensible, not to mention totally impractical, attempt to chip away at *Roe v. Wade* with consent laws, or pro-life propaganda dressed up as counseling for men. It is no surprise that our pathetic excuse for sex education in this country makes little mention of abortion and/or the ways in which men might be affected by it.

* Names listed are pseudonyms.

Abortion's Effect on Men

Very few studies have looked at abortion's effect on men. In general, men report feeling failure, regret, and other emotions following a partner's abortion.

Responses, Prior Events*	
Responses to questions pertaining to events prior to the abortion decision	
Marital Status	Thirty (21%) of 142 respondents said they were married to their partners at the time the abortion occurred.
Contraception	Forty-four (31%) of 141 respondents claimed to have been using birth control prior to pregnancy.
Decision Making	Both partners agreed to obtain abortion = 40 (28%) Man pressured partner to abort = 18 (12%) Other pressured partner to abort = 35 (25%) Man left relationship prior to abortion = 8 (6%) Partner chose to abort against man's wishes = 64 (45%) Man passively left decision to partner = 38 (27%) Man unaware of abortion until after it occurred = 25 (18%)
Reasons for Choosing Abortion	Mental Health/Emotional Distress = 59 (42%) Physical Health = 23 (16%) Financial Concerns = 85 (61%) School/Educational Plans = 67 (48%) Career Plans = 86 (62%) Family Size = 18 (13%) Social Reasons (i.e., embarrassment) = 63 (45%)
Incidence of Post-abortion Problems	Grief/Sadness = 128 Persistent Thoughts About the Baby = 128 Helplessness = 116 Relationship Problems = 115 Anger = 113 Guilt = 112 Isolation = 103 Difficulty Concentrating = 102 Anxiety = 102 Difficulty Sleeping = 91 Sadness at Certain Times of Year = 89 (time of abortion, time of potential birth) Confusion About the Male Role = 87 Sexual Problems = 79 Disturbing Dreams/Nightmares = 77 Increased Risk-Taking = 73 Alcohol/Drug Abuse = 68 Only five respondents did not report any of the problems listed above. Each of these five indicated that they and their partners had agreed to abort. However, 35 of the 40 men who agreed with their partners to abort *did* report experiencing one or more of these problems.

*Note: Respondents were instructed to choose all that apply when responding to the questions concerning abortion decision making and reasons for choosing abortion. Therefore, the percent values indicated for responses to those questions do not add up to 100.

Taken from: Catherine T. Coyle, "An Online Study to Investigate the Effects of Abortion on Men," *Association for Interdisciplinary Research in Values and Social Change Research Bulletin*, vol. 19, no. 1, Winter 2006.

In the clinical sphere, already spread-too-thin therapists and medical staff pay little attention to men's involvement. Ninety-eight percent of clinic counselors are female, so a man hoping to discuss his feelings with a peer is largely out of luck.

In the most comprehensive study of men and abortion to date, Arthur Shostak, a professor of sociology at Drexel University, who describes himself as "unswervingly pro-choice," found that men's single greatest concern was the well-being of their sex partner and, further, that a majority of men would like to accompany their partners throughout the procedure. Most clinics don't allow men beyond the waiting room, something Shostak says is evidence that many think of men as "coat holders and drivers."

Men Deserve a Voice

And in the private sphere, men struggle to reach out to one another about their experiences for a variety of reasons. A stigma against abortion overall remains (more oppressive in some geographies than others, of course), often keeping both women and their partners silent with even the closest of friends and family. In the same way that contemporary men are still groping for ways to be honest with one another about all things sexual—abuse, orientation, dysfunction—they just don't seem to have the language to talk about their abortion experiences.

> **FAST FACT**
>
> In 2008 Ohio and West Virginia considered measures that would restrict women's access to abortion services by requiring consent from or notice to the man involved.

Few young men have fathers or mentors who have authentically modeled opening up about the very common experience of unexpected pregnancy. Wisecracks and silence are still the norm, despite the fact that, according to the Guttmacher Institute, about half of American couples have experienced an unintended pregnancy, and at current rates, more than one-third (35 percent) of women will have had an abortion by age 45.

The pro-choice movement, and feminists in general, seem to have historically shied away from the difficult but imperative task of involving men in conversations about abortion. It is understandable that

The author says that letting men voice their opinions on abortion helps them deal with the event and relieves pregnant women of the burden of being the sole decision maker.

the movement has been weary; no hot-button issue brings out more manipulation than this one. But it is time that feminists' commitment to equality, as well as the quality of both women *and* men's lives, trumps their fear that acknowledging men's hardships will only serve as fodder for pro-life spin doctors. There must be a way to talk about men's perspectives and experiences without compromising women's bodies. . . .

Men's Experiences Count, Too

As more brave voices . . . make their way into both alternative and mainstream media, perhaps boys and men can find a way to enter into dialogue with one another, and with their partners, about how abortion has affected their lives.

There is a growing, though still inadequate, movement to address men's experiences of abortion. At the forefront is Shostak, author of *Men and Abortion, Losses, Lessons, and Loves,* which is based on a survey involving more than a thousand men who responded to questionnaires in the waiting rooms of 30 clinics located in 18 states. Other books are not explicitly aimed at but address men, such as *Unspeakable Losses: Understanding the Experience of Pregnancy Loss, Miscarriage & Abortion*, by Kim Kluger-Bell, and *The Choices We Made*, by Angela Bonavoglia. Online, pro choice men can find support at www.menandabortion.com, a site founded in 2006 and still in development.

There is a price to both men and women when men don't feel supported or safe to talk about their experiences with a partner's abortions. Men can be pushed further into anxious masculinity, subconsciously convinced that if the world acts like their feelings don't matter, they'll just pretend not to have them. Women are then burdened with both the physical responsibility of the abortion *and* the entire emotional responsibility of processing what it means.

If both men and women feel like they have a role in the procedure and healing—however that's interpreted by partners, depending on their spiritual and/or political beliefs—we will be healthier as a whole. Perhaps men, freed from the shackles of silence, will also be more prone to help out in the important work of keeping *Roe v. Wade* intact and abortion safer and less stigmatized for everyone.

EVALUATING THE AUTHOR'S ARGUMENTS:

Martin says that men suffer from abortion down the road because they are denied "the ritual of that choice." Explain in your own words what you think she means by this. What does the ritual of choice mean to you? What do you think it might mean to men who have impregnated a woman?

Viewpoint

4

Women Should Not Have to Consider Men's Feelings When Considering Abortion

"Men have feelings, too! Of course they do. But they don't have uteruses."

Catherine Price

In the following viewpoint Catherine Price argues that women should be the primary decision makers about abortion since it is a decision that involves their bodies. She discusses a recent trend among men who claim to be so scarred by their lovers' abortions that they talk about the procedure as if it happened to them personally. Price rejects this suggestion—the only person who can experience an abortion is a woman, and thus her feelings on the matter are more important. Price understands that men may have strong emotions about abortion, but she criticizes pro-life movements that convince men they are as involved in abortion as women. In Price's eyes, they are not, and it is wrong for men to co-opt this important women's issue.

Catherine Price, "It's My Abortion, Too!" Salon.com, January 8, 2008. This article first appeared in Salon.com, at http://www.salon.com. An online version remains in the Salon archives. Reprinted with permission.

Catherine Price is a writer whose work has appeared in the *New York Times, Men's Journal,* and on Salon.com, where this viewpoint was originally published.

AS YOU READ, CONSIDER THE FOLLOWING QUESTIONS:

1. Who is Mark B. Morrow, and how does he factor into the author's argument?
2. Why, in the author's opinion, is it wrong to use men's grief as a weapon in the fight against abortion?
3. In what way does the author say national conferences on men and abortion take advantage of men's complicated feelings on abortion?

Jan. 08, 2008| Traditionally, the fight over abortion has focused on the woman and her fetus, with the father relegated to the sidelines, if mentioned at all. No longer. According to a piece in the *Los Angeles Times* called "Changing Abortion's Pronoun," there's a growing movement of "positive-abortive fathers" who claim that abortion's "pronoun is all wrong."

"*We* had abortions," one of the men—who was responsible for four pregnancies that ended in abortion—is quoted as saying. "I've had abortions."

That man—Mark B. Morrow—is a Christian counselor who recently spoke at a conference in San Francisco that was supposedly the first national conference on men and abortion. It featured, among other things, personal testimony from men who claimed that their lovers' abortions left them scarred. Some became depressed; others nursed their sorrow with alcohol, or had obsessive dreams about their imaginary relationships with children who were never born. Looking back over their lives and the abortions, these men feel a sense of regret so profound, they say, that they've decided to join the fight against abortion, using not violence but, as the article puts it, "the power of men's tears."

I don't mean to sound insensitive, but I have to say that this whole thing creeps me out. The most obvious argument against this pronoun shift, of course, is that it's medically inaccurate—maybe I missed

A man protests against abortion in San Francisco, California. The author says that while men are entitled to have feelings about abortion, they shouldn't be involved in a woman's decision to have one.

something in health class, but I don't think you can have an abortion unless you have the capacity to give birth. By altering the pronoun to include the father, these men want to assume ownership over something that is anatomically impossible, not to mention conflate the two very different issues of physical and emotional ownership. I can hear the men's response: But that ignores our emotions! Men have feelings, too! Of course they do. But they don't have uteruses.

I think few people would argue that the decision to have an abortion is a serious one, and that it carries the possibility of regret. There are plenty of instances when both women and men could benefit from therapy or counseling both before and after the abortion—and it is definitely not a decision to be taken lightly. But to use men's grief over unborn children as a weapon in the fight against abortion seems to miss the point—it has nothing to do with the fetus. I thought that the main opposition to abortion had to do with the "murder" of the would-be baby, not with whether the dad might stay up nights wishing his partner hadn't terminated the pregnancy.

What's more, the strong emotions that can come in the wake of an abortion do not mean that the decision was wrong, or something to feel guilty about. In some men's cases, this movement seems to take advantage of a natural grieving process. Instead of helping men work through this grief—and in some cases regret—and move on with their lives, it convinces them that they're abortion victims themselves and that they have a moral obligation to fight it. When this manipulation gets mixed up with Jesus talk, I get even more uncomfortable. As the article puts it:

> Recruits often cycle through church-based retreats, support groups and Bible studies that aim to heal post-abortion trauma. The men are urged to think of themselves as fathers, to name—and ask forgiveness from—the children they might have raised, had their partners not aborted.

At one retreat, the men are told to picture their sons and daughters dancing in a sunny meadow at the feet of Jesus Christ.

"They draw in men who may have a little ambivalence, possibly a little guilt, and they exacerbate those feelings," [sociologist Arthur] Shostak said.

Last, this victimization of the would-be dads seems to border

FAST FACT

According to the Alan Guttmacher Institute, more than two-thirds of all abortions are performed on women who have never been married.

on narcissism—a self-absorption that has less to do with the fetuses or the mothers or the actual abortions and more to do simply with the men themselves. Take, for example, a 50-year-old man described in the article who was responsible for two pregnancies that ended in abortion. He has since converted to Catholicism, has five children, and sometimes protests outside abortion clinics. He regrets the abortions and is in an ongoing intellectual debate with himself over whether the two unborn children were necessary for him to have the life—and family—he has today. But when asked what his ex-girlfriends might think about the effect the abortions had on *their* lives, the man looked startled, the article reports. "I never really thought about it for the woman," he told the *Times.*

To me, at least, that's a problem.

EVALUATING THE AUTHORS' ARGUMENTS:

In this viewpoint Catherine Price argues that men should not be involved in a woman's decision to have an abortion. In the previous viewpoint Courtney E. Martin argues they should. Both authors of these opposing viewpoints are women—does this surprise you? If so, why? If not, why not? After reading both viewpoints, explain what role you think men should play in a woman's decision to have an abortion.

Women Have a Right to Access Birth Control

Sarah Carey

"*Doctors won't give up the morning-after pill because they want to give the safe-sex lecture. Well thanks, but I've had enough of the lectures. I am responsible for my own fertility and I'd like to be able to buy the pill.*"

In the following viewpoint Sarah Carey argues that women need to be able to access birth control without having to pay a lot of money, travel long distances, or get the consent of their doctor. Though both men and women engage in sex, Carey says only women have the possibility of getting accidentally pregnant from the act. Therefore, to protect their bodies from unwanted pregnancy, they need to be able to access birth control with the fewest number of obstacles possible. She charges doctors and politicians who want restrictions put on birth control with seeking to control women's behavior and to make them feel bad about their choices. Carey concludes there is no reason why women should have to get permission from anyone to protect their bodies from unwanted pregnancies.

Sarah Carey writes frequently for the *Times*, a London newspaper in which this article originally appeared.

AS YOU READ, CONSIDER THE FOLLOWING QUESTIONS:
  1. What, according to Carey, is "humiliating" for women?
  2. Who uses contraception the least, according to Carey?
  3. What does the word *protectionism* mean in the context of the viewpoint?

I'm not pregnant. Thank God. I was worried for a couple of weeks, though. I felt dizzy one day and my mother immediately leapt to conclusions. Then the PMT [premenstrual tension] set in, but every PMT symptom can be interpreted as a pregnancy symptom and I was getting paranoid.

Phew! We're just emerging from the two-babies-in-two-years fog and I am not sure I could have stood up, physically or mentally, to another one. My husband says he'd have left the country. Thankfully he can remain here and ferry up my tea and toast in the morning.

Birth Control Access Is Critical for Women

It was a close call, though, and enough to get me exercised when I read the patronising comments of Martin Daly, chairman of the Irish Medical Organisation's GP [general practitioner] Committee, [in October 2006]. Dr Daly believes that the morning-after pill should not be distributed by pharmacies; prescribing it should remain the preserve of GPs.

Well, I bet Dr Daly never woke up on a Saturday morning wondering if he was pregnant and realising that he couldn't get his hands on the solution to his problem until Monday morning, when it might be too late. Funny how those who never have to face a problem can confidently assure the rest of us that there isn't one.

Women Don't Need Lectures—They Need Help

I'd had a close call on a Friday night and when I woke up I had a choice. Do I spend three weeks panicking or take a morning-after pill and eliminate the anxiety? Actually, I didn't have a choice because my GP doesn't open on a Saturday. He only opens on a Monday, Wednesday and Friday between 10am and 12.

It's bad enough when you get into the surgery [doctor's office]; it's so humiliating. You have to give the "details" of the "incident". You may have to explain to the receptionist why you must see the doctor that day and no other. So much for confidentiality.

Then the doctor gets to shake his patrician head at your silliness and gives you a contraception lecture. Possibly justifiable when I was 18 and drunk. Now I'm 35 and just tired. Give me the stupid pill and spare me the lecture. Oh, and here's your $50 even though you haven't had to do anything since I told you what was wrong with me and what I need.

Doctors Exert Control over Women

There's the rub. It's a nice little earner: a steady queue [line] of healthy women coming into your office requiring nothing other than your signature and your disapproval for which you get handsomely paid. Hardly surprising that Dr Daly doesn't want to let go of that revenue stream. Naturally he'll deny that finance is the source of his concern. It's not just the money—it's the control.

"We believe that the vast majority of women who seek it are in their late teens and early 20s and the opportunity should be taken to explain that emergency contraception is just that," Daly said. "It's a last resort." He wants to talk to the women about "the implications of being sexually active and how to protect against sexually transmitted diseases".

Quite frankly he's wrong—on all counts. Firstly, regardless of age, if a woman is responsible enough to look for the pill in the first place then I think it's fair to assume that she is quite well aware of the "implications" of being sexually active. Secondly, there was a lot of fuss about a survey on Irish

FAST FACT

A 2004 CBS News/*New York Times* poll found that 78 percent of Americans believe religious pharmacists should not be able to refuse to sell birth control pills to women who have a prescription for them.

people's sexual habits a fortnight [two weeks] ago. Most media head-lined the highly predictable fact that young people are having lots of sex with lots of different people. Dr Daly might have found the section on

Birth Control Options for Women

Advocates argue that women have many methods of birth control to prevent unwanted pregnancies.

Methods	Number of Pregnancies Expected per 100 Women	How to Use it	Some Risks
Implantable Rod	1	One-time procedure; nothing to do or remember	◆ Acne ◆ Weight gain ◆ Cysts of the ovaries ◆ Mood changes ◆ Depression ◆ Hair loss ◆ Headache ◆ Upset stomach ◆ Dizziness ◆ Sore breasts
IUD	1	One-time procedure; nothing to do or remember	◆ Cramps ◆ Bleeding ◆ Pelvic inflammatory disease ◆ Infertility ◆ Tear or hole in the uterus ◆ Lower interest in sexual activity ◆ Changes in period
Shot/ Injection	1	Need a shot every 3 months	◆ Bone loss ◆ Bleeding between periods ◆ Weight gain ◆ Breast tenderness ◆ Headaches
Oral Contraceptives (Combined Pill) "The Pill"	5	Must swallow a pill every day	◆ Dizziness ◆ Nausea ◆ Changes in cycle (period) ◆ Changes in mood ◆ Weight gain ◆ High blood pressure ◆ Blood clots ◆ Heart attack ◆ Strokes
Oral Contraceptives (Progestin-only) "The Pill"	5	Must swallow a pill every day	◆ Irregular bleeding ◆ Weight gain ◆ Breast tenderness
Oral Contraceptives Extended/ Continuous Use "The Pill"	5	Must swallow a pill every day	◆ Risks are similar to other oral contraceptives ◆ Bleeding ◆ Spotting between periods

Methods	Number of Pregnancies Expected per 100 Women	How to Use it	Some Risks
Patch	5	Must wear a patch every day	◆ Exposure to higher average levels of estrogen than most oral contraceptives
Vaginal Contraceptive Ring	5	Must leave ring in every day for 3 weeks	◆ Vaginal discharge ◆ Swelling of the vagina ◆ Irritation ◆ Similar to oral contraceptives
Male Condom	11–16	Must use every time you have sex; requires partner's cooperation. Except for abstinence, latex condoms are the best protection against HIV/AIDS and other STIs	◆ Allergic reactions
Diaphragm with Spermicide	15	Must use every time you have sex	◆ Irritation ◆ Allergic reactions ◆ Urinary tract infection ◆ Toxic shock
Sponge with Spermicide	16–32	Must use every time you have sex	◆ Irritation ◆ Allergic reactions ◆ Hard time removing ◆ Toxic shock
Cervical Cap with Spermicide	17–23	Must use every time you have sex	◆ Irritation ◆ Allergic reactions ◆ Abnormal Pap test ◆ Toxic shock
Female Condom	20	Must use every time you have sex. May give some protection against STIs	◆ Irritation ◆ Allergic reactions
Spermicide	30	Must use every time you have sex	◆ Irritation ◆ Allergic reactions ◆ Urinary tract infection
Emergency Contraception – if your primary method of birth control fails			
Emergency Contraceptives "The Morning-After Pill"	15	Must use within 72 hours of unprotected sex. It should not be used as a regular form of birth control	◆ Nausea ◆ Vomiting ◆ Abdominal pain ◆ Fatigue ◆ Headache

contraception interesting: some 90% of the allegedly slutty teenagers he wants to talk to about "the implications of sexual activity" are using contraception.

Guess who is using the least? Married women aged 35–44. These are women sick of being dosed with artificial hormones and who believe that their fertility is low enough not to warrant using contraception. Perhaps they believe they have low fertility because they read headlines screeching about women who postpone child-bearing until their thirties when their fertility has dropped to disastrous levels.

The bottom line is that doctors won't give up the morning-after pill because they want to give the safe-sex lecture. Well thanks, but I've had enough of the lectures. I am responsible for my own fertility and I'd like to be able to buy the pill in a chemist [pharmacy] without the moralizing.

Don't Place Extra Burdens on Women

I see that the Irish Family Planning Association opened an emergency contraception clinic in Tallaght. Guess who's going to it? People from Carlow and Kildare. It makes no sense for people to travel these distances to get a pill they could just as easily get in their local chemist.

Levonelle, the brand name of the pill, has only been available in this country since June 2003. Prior to that the "morning-after pill" that doctors were lowering themselves to hand out was just a double dose of the normal pill, though they didn't like you to know that.

"In the UK, the NHS [National Health Service] has gone down the route of making it available over the counter for the past five years and it has made no difference," Daly said. Difference to what? Pregnancy rates? Well, obviously, those who don't think they need the pill are still going to get pregnant. For those who know they need it, why make it as difficult and expensive as possible to get? $50–$80 is a lot of money. Cheaper than being pregnant and cheaper than a flight to London for an abortion. But enough to put someone off, especially when they aren't certain if the risk warrants the inconvenience, the mortification and the investment.

Daly again: "If there was a clear-cut advantage to making it available over the counter, I would consider it but so far there has been

The author says women should have access to the morning-after pill and should not have to see a doctor or endure a lecture just to protect themselves from unwanted pregnancies.

none." Well, there is no clear-cut advantage to him obviously, but there would be to panic-stricken women.

It Is a Woman's Right to Access Safe Birth Control

Why not just dispense it in a pharmacy? Their opening hours are better and it would be cheaper. There could always be some deal whereby they tell your GP that you came in for it, and an obligation on them to give you a leaflet on non-emergency contraception.

Most disappointingly Mary Harney, the health minister, hasn't the slightest intention of putting pressure on doctors to let go this control over women. "Clearly, it can only be done if it's medically safe to do so and until we get the advice of the regulatory body that has responsibility in this area, I wouldn't be in a position to make a decision," she has said.

But it is medically safe. Safe as houses. It's so safe that breast-feeding women can take it, and they aren't allowed to take an anti-histamine. This has nothing to do with safety. It's just old-fashioned protectionism by the establishment to defend their income and their status.

EVALUATING THE AUTHOR'S ARGUMENTS:

Sarah Carey quotes from several sources to support the points she makes in her essay. Make a list of everyone she quotes, including their credentials and the nature of their comments. Then, analyze her sources—are they credible? Are they well qualified to speak on this subject?

Women Should Not Always Have a Right to Access Birth Control

Jay Johansen

"Just because something is legal doesn't mean that others are obligated to help you do it."

In the following viewpoint Jay Johansen argues that women should not have the right to access birth control if the pharmacist dispensing the birth control does not approve of the medication's use. Johansen says that many pharmacists take issue with certain forms of birth control, and it is a violation of their rights to be forced to dispense these to someone—it amounts to participating in a murder, for them. If a pharmacist does not want to dispense birth control, says Johansen, a woman may obtain it from many other sources—her doctor, another pharmacy, or even another pharmacist at the same store. Because women have these options, Johansen says it is acceptable for pharmacists to refuse to fill a prescription for birth control that conflicts with their moral principles.

Jay Johansen writes about issues concerning pharmacists for the Web site PregnantPause.com.

AS YOU READ, CONSIDER THE FOLLOWING QUESTIONS:
1. California, Missouri, and New Jersey each have considered passing what kind of law, according to the author?
2. What do gas stations and cigarettes have to do with pharmacists and birth control, according to Johansen?
3. In what way does the author suggest pharmacies are similar to Kentucky Fried Chicken restaurants and Ford dealerships?

Should a pharmacist be required to fill any prescription brought to him?

Governor [Rod] Blagojevich of Illinois says yes. In April of 2005 he issued an executive order requiring pharmacists to fill any legal prescription. As of this writing, three states—California, Missouri, and New Jersey—are considering laws to this effect, and such a law has been proposed in Congress.

What even prompts such a law? Why would a pharmacist *not* want to fill a prescription? Well, some pharmacists have religious or moral objections to birth control, especially to forms of birth control that can cause very early abortions. They don't want anything to do with what they believe is the killing of an innocent baby.

Pharmacists Have Rights, Too

Prevention magazine printed an article they entitled "Access Denied". While they made an effort to give some balance and present both sides, they came down on the side of requiring pharmacists to fill prescriptions even if they have moral objections. After giving some lip service to the concerns of a pharmacist who does not want to be a party to something he considers immoral, they ask, "But at what point does personal belief undermine public health? If more women lose access to hormonal contraceptives, rates of unintended pregnancy and abortions will rise in the US, predicts Beth Jordan, MD, medical director of the Washington, DC–based Feminist Majority Foundation. . . . What's more, oral contraceptives aren't only used to prevent pregnancy. The Pill may cut the risk of ovarian cancer by up to 80 percent and is used by women at high genetic risk for this hard-to-detect and usually fatal cancer."

(It is certainly touching to hear that the Femnist Majority Foundation, an outspoken pro-abortion group, is concerned that something might cause an increase in the abortion rate. This is a little like the National Rifle Association wringing its hands in concern that some proposed legislation might result in more people buying guns.)

The American Pharmacist Association took issue with the *Prevention* article. "Pharmacists and physicians who refuse to provide access to oral contraceptives are painted the villains in an article in the current issue

There has been much controversy over some pharmacists' refusal to dispense birth control on moral and religious grounds.

of *Prevention* magazine, read by 10 million Americans each month. The article fails to portray accurately pharmacists' rights of conscience. . . ." They proposed a compromise: Pharmacists should have the right to "step away but not step in the way". They explained that what they meant by this was ". . . when a pharmacist has a moral or ethical dilemma with dispensing any product, another pharmacist on duty can fill the prescription, the patient can be sent to a pharmacy that will provide the therapy, or other mechanisms can be established." But note that even their proposed compromise requires the objecting pharmacist to help the patient get this prescription filled.

The American Medical Association went a step further. They passed a resolution stating that they "support legislation that requires individual pharmacists or pharmacy chains to fill legally valid prescriptions or to provide immediate referral to an appropriate alternative dispensing pharmacy without interference . . . if an individual pharmacist exercises a conscientious refusal to dispense a legal prescription, a patient's right to obtain legal prescriptions will be protected by immediate referral to an appropriate dispensing pharmacy." This theoretically affirms the pharmacist's rights of conscience, but all the guarantees are on the other side.

Women Have Plenty of Ways to Get Birth Control

In short, the argument for requiring pharmacists to fill such prescriptions is that patients have a legal right to have these prescriptions filled, and for a pharmacist to refuse to fill one violates the rights of the patient. Advocates of these "must fill" policies or laws regularly point out that contraceptives and abortifacients [a substance that induces an abortion] are legal, and that this makes the moral objections of the pharmacist irrelevant.

But surely just because something is legal doesn't mean that others are obligated to help you do it. I have yet to hear this line of reasoning applied to any other product someone might want to buy. Like, "It is legal (for adults) to buy pornography. Therefore, every bookstore should be required to sell pornography. For a bookstore to refuse to sell a customer pornography would violate the customer's rights." Or, should every gas station be required to sell cigarettes? Does the fact that cigarettes are legal mean that a gas station owner with moral objections to smoking has no right to place obstacles in the way of smokers by refusing to carry cigarettes?

Indeed, retailers routinely decide not to stock products for all sorts of reasons. Kentucky Fried Chicken doesn't sell pizza. My local Ford dealer doesn't sell Chryslers. My local grocery store doesn't sell any used cars at all. Should we have laws to require every store to carry every legal product that exists in the world?

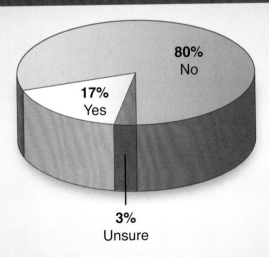

Should Pharmacists Be Allowed to Refuse to Sell Birth Control?

At least some Americans believe pharmacists should be able to refuse to dispense birth control pills to women if it conflicts with their beliefs.

Question: Should pharmacists be able to refuse to sell birth control?

80%
No

17%
Yes

3%
Unsure

Taken from: Pew Research Center for the People and the Press and Pew Forum on Religion and Public Life, 2006.

Not a Violation of Patient's Rights

How does any of this violate the patient's rights? If a pharmacist refuses to fill certain types of prescriptions, there are surely other pharmacists who will be happy to take the business. No one is even suggesting that these pharmacists tried to prevent patients from getting their prescriptions somewhere else.

Interestingly enough, *Prevention* magazine doesn't even apply this logic to their own web site. They have forums where readers may post comments, but they include a long list of types of comments that they will not accept, including anything "harmful, threatening, abusive, harassing, tortious, defamatory, sexist, vulgar, obscene, libelous, invasive of another's privacy, hateful, or racially, ethnically or otherwise objectionable". Some of these things are illegal, but most are not. So just because something is legal doesn't mean they will post it on their web site. Why not? Why don't they want sexist, vulgar, or racist comments on their web site? Surely it is because they have moral objections to such things. If they have the right to refuse to be a party to conduct that violates their moral standards, why shouldn't pharmacists have that same right?

EVALUATING THE AUTHORS' ARGUMENTS:

Johansen argues that if a woman encounters a pharmacist who does not want to fill her birth control prescription, she can just find another pharmacist who will. How do you think each of the authors in this chapter might respond to this suggestion? Use evidence from the viewpoints in your answer. Then, state whether you think pharmacists should have the right to refuse to fill patients' prescriptions.

Facts About Women's Rights

Editor's note: These facts can be used in reports or papers to reinforce or add credibility when making important points or claims.

Facts About Women in Politics

The Center for Women in Politics reports the following about women who hold political office in the United States:

- In 2009, ninety women held positions in the U.S. Congress.
- Seventeen women held office in the Senate.
- Seventy-three women served in the House of Representatives.
- In 2007, Democratic senator Nancy Pelosi became the first woman to hold the position of Speaker of the House.
- There were eight female governors in the United States in 2009. They presided over the states of Alaska, Arizona, Connecticut, Hawaii, Kansas, Michigan, North Carolina, and Washington.

As of 2009 the top ten states with the highest percentage of female legislators were:

- Colorado (39 percent)
- Vermont (37.2 percent)
- New Hampshire (37 percent)
- Minnesota (34.8 percent)
- Hawaii (32.9 percent)
- Washington (32 percent)
- Nevada (31.7 percent)
- Connecticut (31.6 percent)
- Maryland (31.4 percent)
- Arizona (31.1 percent)

According to the International Parliamentary Union (IPU):

- In 2005, the rate of female representation around the world stood at nearly 16 percent.

- One-fifth of the world's parliamentarians elected in 2005 were women, according to a report released in February 2006.
- Just 11 of 187 countries listed with the IPU have no women in parliament: Bahrain, Kyrgyzstan, Micronesia, Nauru, Nepal, Palau, Saint Kitts and Nevis, Saudi Arabia, Solomon Islands, Tuvalu, and the United Arab Emirates.
- Of the thirty-nine countries that held elections in 2005, the numbers of women in parliament increased in twenty-eight of them.

As of February 2006, women made up more than 30 percent of parliamentary bodies in twenty countries:
- Rwanda (48.8 percent of parliament was female)
- Sweden (45.3 percent)
- Norway (37.9 percent)
- Finland (37.5 percent)
- Denmark (36.9 percent)
- Netherlands (36.7 percent)
- Cuba (36.0 percent)
- Spain (36.0 percent)
- Costa Rica (35.1 percent)
- Argentina (35.0 percent)
- Mozambique (34.8 percent)
- Belgium (34.7 percent)
- Austria (33.9 percent)
- Iceland (33.3 percent)
- South Africa (32.8 percent)
- New Zealand (32.2 percent)
- Germany (31.8 percent)
- Guyana (30.8 percent)
- Burundi (30.5 percent)
- Tanzania (30.4 percent)

Facts About Women and Work
In 2007 the U.S. Department of Labor reported the following about women and work:
- Seventy-one million (or 59.3 percent) of U.S. women were working or looking for work.

- Women made up 46 percent of the total U.S. workforce.
- By 2016 women are expected to make up 47 percent of the labor force.
- Women are expected to account for 49 percent of the increase in total labor-force growth between 2006 and 2016.
- Seventy-five percent of employed women work full time.
- Twenty-five percent of employed women work part time.
- Sixty-eight million women are employed in the United States.

The ten highest-paying full-time occupations held by women are:
- Pharmacist, $1,603 (median weekly earning)
- Chief executive, $1,536
- Lawyer, $1,381
- Computer and information systems manager, $1,363
- Computer software engineer, $1,318
- Psychologist, $1,152
- Physical therapist, $1,096
- Management analyst, $1,083
- Computer programmer, $1,074
- Human resource manager, $1,073

The American Federation of Labor and Congress of Industrial Organizations reports the following about women who worked in 2006:
- Of women who work, 43.6 percent belong to a labor union.
- Women in unions earn about 30.9 percent more than women who are not members of a union.
- About 13.8 percent of women do not have health insurance.
- Approximately 14.1 percent of women in the United States live in poverty.
- Of women over age sixty-five, 78 percent rely on Social Security for half or more of their income.
- Of women sixty-five and older with income, 23.1 percent receive a pension.

According to the U.S. Census Bureau:
- Women in Washington, D.C., earned ninety-one cents for every dollar that men earned in 2004.

- The five sectors in which women's median earnings equaled $40,000 or more were management of companies and enterprises ($41,608); mining ($41,516); professional, scientific, and technical services ($41,398); utilities ($40,981); and information ($40,447).
- Women earned 90 percent or more of what men did in the following professions: installation, maintenance, and repair; community and social services; construction and extraction; and health care support.
- Women earned 65 percent of what men did in the following fields: legal, sales and related occupations, health care practitioners, and technical professions.

According to a study conducted by McGill University:
- The United States, Lesotho, Liberia, Swaziland, and Papua New Guinea were the only countries out of 173 studied that did not guarantee paid maternity leave.
- Of the 168 countries that do offer paid maternity leave, 98 offered fourteen or more weeks of paid time off.

Under the Family and Medical Leave Act of 1993, U.S. workers are allowed to take up to twelve weeks of unpaid leave for maternity, family, and other medical needs.

According to the United Nations, maternity leave around the world breaks down as follows:
- Afghanistan: Ninety days at 100 percent of pay
- Algeria: Fourteen weeks at 100 percent of pay
- Austria: Sixteen weeks at 100 percent of pay
- China: Ninety days at 100 percent of pay
- Congo: Fifteen weeks at 100 percent of pay
- Cuba: Eighteen weeks at 100 percent of pay
- Iceland: Ninety days at 80 percent of pay
- India: Twelve weeks at 100 percent of pay
- Iran: Ninety days at 67 percent of pay
- Iraq: Sixty-two days at 100 percent of pay
- Israel: Twelve weeks up to 100 percent of pay (with ceiling)

- Italy: Five months at 80 percent of pay
- Mexico: Twelve weeks at 100 percent of pay
- Morocco: Fourteen weeks at 100 percent of pay
- United Kingdom: Twenty-six weeks at 90 percent of pay for first six weeks with a flat rate thereafter

Facts About Violence Against Women in the United States

According to the Family Violence and Prevention Fund:
- One in five female high-school students has been physically and/or sexually abused by a date.
- Eight percent of high-school girls report they have been forced to have sex with their boyfriend.
- Forty percent of girls aged fourteen to seventeen report knowing a girl their age who has been hit by her boyfriend.

The National Center for Injury Prevention and Control reports that 4.8 million women in the United States experience partner-inflicted physical assaults and rapes.

According to the Bureau of Justice, 1,181 women were murdered by their partners in 2005—equal to about three murders every day.

In 2008 the National Network to End Domestic Violence conducted a twenty-four-hour survey of domestic violence shelters and services and found:
- More than twenty thousand adult and child victims of abuse sought refuge in emergency shelters.
- More than ten thousand adult and child abuse victims were living in transitional housing.
- Nearly nine thousand requests for assistance went unmet because of a lack of funding.

Facts About Muslim Women Around the World

The United Nations Population Fund estimates that five thousand women are killed each year in honor killings, though most experts agree the figure is actually much higher.

A 2005 Gallup poll of the Muslim world found the following percentages of Muslim women who said they were able to make their own voting decisions:

- 97 percent (Lebanon)
- 95 percent (Egypt)
- 95 percent (Morocco)
- 94 percent (Turkey)
- 92 percent (Iran)
- 78 percent (Jordan)
- 69 percent (Saudi Arabia)
- 68 percent (Pakistan)
- The same poll found that: In Turkey, 92 percent of men and women believed women should have equal rights.
- In Morocco, 51 percent of men and 87 percent of women believed in equal rights for men and women.

Organizations to Contact

The editors have compiled the following list of organizations concerned with the issues debated in this book. The descriptions are derived from materials provided by the organizations. All have publications or information available for interested readers. The list was compiled on the date of publication of the present volume; the information provided here may change. Be aware that many organizations take several weeks or longer to respond to queries, so allow as much time as possible.

Alan Guttmacher Institute
125 Maiden Ln., New York, NY 10038
e-mail: info@agi-usa.org
Web site: www.agi-usa.org

The institute works to protect and expand the reproductive choices of all women and men. It provides women the information and services they need to exercise their rights and responsibilities concerning sexual activity, reproduction, and family planning. Among the institute's publications are the books *Emergency Contraception Has Tremendous Potential in the Fight to Reduce Unintended Pregnancy* and *Striking a Balance Between a Provider's Right to Refuse and a Patient's Right to Receive Care.*

American Association of University Women (AAUW)
1111 Sixteenth St. NW, Washington, D.C. 20036
(202) 785-7700
e-mail: info@aauw.org
Web site: www.aauw.org

This national organization promotes education and workplace equity for all women and girls. For more than 127 years, AAUW members have examined and taken positions on the fundamental issues of the day—educational, social, economic, and political.

Catholics for a Free Choice

1436 U St. NW, Ste. 301, Washington, D.C. 20009
e-mail: cffc@catholicsforchoice.org
Web site: www.cath4choice.org

This organization promotes family planning to reduce the need for abortion and to increase women's choice in childbearing and child rearing. It publishes the bimonthly newsletter *Conscience*.

Center for the American Woman and Politics (CAWP)

Eagleton Institute on Politics at Rutgers University
191 Ryders Ln., New Brunswick, NJ 08901-8557
Web site: www.cawp.rutgers.edu

The Center for American Women and Politics, a unit of the Eagleton Institute of Politics at Rutgers, is a leading source of scholarly research and data about American women in politics. The CAWP collects facts on women in politics, tracks women running for electoral office, and analyzes presidential election results. The CAWP also runs the nationally recognized Pathways to Politics program—a two-week camp—where Girl Scouts learn about women in politics.

The Feminist Majority

433 S. Beverly Dr., Beverly Hills, CA 90212
Web site: http://feminist.org

The organization encourages women to fill leadership positions in business, education, media, law, medicine, and government. It sponsors projects and a speakers bureau and compiles statistics on women in leadership roles. The fund publishes the quarterly *Feminist Majority Report* as well as a newsletter, fact sheets, books, and videos.

Legal Momentum

395 Hudson St., New York, NY 10014
Web site: www.legalmomentum.org

Formerly the NOW Legal Defense and Education Fund, Legal Momentum is the oldest legal advocacy organization dedicated to advancing the rights of women and girls in the United States. The organization litigates and establishes public policy strategies to promote equality and justice for women and girls. It currently focuses on liberating women and girls from violence and works to promote equal work for equal pay, good health care, and strong, supportive families and communities.

National Abortion and Reproductive Rights Action League (NARAL)

1556 Fifteenth St. NW, Ste. 700, Washington, D.C. 20005
e-mail: comments@naral.org
Web site: www.prochoiceamerica.org

NARAL is the nation's leading advocate for privacy and a woman's right to affordable birth control. NARAL works to protect the pro-choice values of freedom and privacy while reducing the need for abortions. It publishes numerous articles, pamphlets, reports, and news briefs about the state of women's access to birth control in America.

National Association of Women Business Owners

1511 K St. NW, Ste. 1100, Washington, D.C. 20005
(202) 638-5322
Web site: www.nawbo.org

The National Association of Women Business Owners is the unified voice of America's more than 10 million women-owned businesses. The organization offers leadership training and a network for women who have been in business for themselves for more than eight years.

National Organization for Women (NOW)

1000 Sixteenth St. NW, Ste. 700, Washington, D.C. 20036
Web site: www.now.org

With chapters in all fifty states plus the District of Columbia, NOW is one of the largest and most influential feminist organizations in the United States. NOW has more than 550,000 members in 550 chapters across the United States. It seeks to end prejudice and discrimination against women in all areas of life. NOW lobbies legislatures to make laws more equitable and works to educate and inform the public on women's issues. It publishes the *NOW Times,* a newspaper, policy statements, and articles.

National Right to Life Committee (NRLC)
512 Tenth St. NW, Washington, D.C. 20004
(202) 626-8800
Web site: www.nrlc.org

The NRLC is one of the largest organizations opposing abortion. The committee campaigns against legislation to legalize or reduce restrictions on abortion. Its Web site provides information on its ongoing efforts and a link to its publication *National Right to Life News.*

National Women's Political Caucus (NWPC)
1211 Connecticut Ave. NW, Ste. 425, Washington, D.C. 20036
(202) 785-1100
Web site: www.nwpc.org

This multipartisan, multicultural organization is dedicated to increasing women's participation in the political field and creating a political power base designed to achieve equality for all women. Through recruiting, training, and financial donations, the NWPC provides support to women candidates running for all levels of office regardless of political affiliation.

Planned Parenthood Federation of America
434 W. Thirty-third St., New York, NY 10011
e-mail: communications@ppfa.org
Web site: www.plannedparenthood.org

Planned Parenthood believes individuals have the right to control their own fertility without governmental interference. It promotes comprehensive sex education and provides contraceptive counseling and services through clinics across the United States.

Women's Environment and Development Organization (WEDO)
355 Lexington Ave., 3rd Fl., New York, NY 10017
(212) 973-0325
Web site: www.wedo.org

WEDO was established in 1990 by former U.S. congresswoman Bella Abzug (1920–1998) and feminist activist and journalist Mim Kelber (1922–2004). Since its inception, WEDO has been a leader in organizing women for international conferences and actions. In 1992 WEDO organized the World Women's Congress for a Healthy Planet, bringing together more than fifteen hundred women from eighty-three countries to work jointly on a strategy for the UN Conference on Environment and Development.

Women's Forum Against Fundamentalism in Iran (WFAFI)

PO Box 15205, Boston, MA 02215
e-mail: info@wfafi.org
Web site: www.fafi.org

The Women's Forum Against Fundamentalism in Iran works to promote awareness of the special challenges women face living in fundamentalist Iran. The WFAFI seeks to promote public awareness through research projects and outreach programs as well as policy discussions and analysis. According to WFAFI's mission statement, "We firmly believe the political presence, participation and leadership of women are instrumental to achieving social, political and economic equality."

The Women's Rights Project (WRP)

125 Broad St., 18th Fl., New York, NY 10004-2400
Web site: www.aclu.org/reproductiverights

The Women's Rights Project was founded in 1972 by Ruth Bader Ginsburg. Since that time it has focused on legal battles to ensure women's rights in education and employment and has been an active participant in nearly all major gender-discrimination cases that reached the Supreme Court. The WRP advocates for victims of domestic violence as well as for women and girls in the criminal justice system.

Worldwide Islamic Network of Women (WINOW)

e-mail: info@islamwomen.org
Web site: www.islamwomen.org

WINOW is an online global community for Muslim women. It provides news and information for and about the Muslim community and offers guidance for women of Islam in marriage, family, raising children, human rights, religious practice, and scripture.

For Further Reading

Books

Karen E. Bender, et al. *Choice: True Stories of Birth, Contraception, Infertility, Adoption, Single Parenthood, and Abortion.* San Francisco: McAdam/Cage, 2007. This book explores the issue of reproductive choice in a series of twenty-two essays by various authors. It seeks to highlight reproductive choices and obstacles sexually active women must face in their daily lives.

Francine D. Blau, Marianne A. Ferber, and Anne E. Winkler. *The Economics of Women, Men, and Work.* Upper Saddle River, NJ: Prentice Hall, 2005. The authors examine the roles of men and women in the workplace.

Julie Ann Dolan. *Women and Politics: Paths to Power and Political Influence.* Upper Saddle River, NJ: Prentice Hall, 2006. This work provides an account of the contribution of women in positions of power in politics, the media, and the judicial system.

Warren Farrell. *Why Men Earn More: The Startling Truth Behind the Pay Gap.* New York: AMACOM, 2005. The author argues that men earn more money than women because they deserve to—men take on high-risk, dangerous jobs, work longer hours, and get more profitable degrees.

Linda Gordon. *The Moral Property of Women: A History of Birth Control Politics in America.* Chicago: University of Illinois Press, 2007. This book analyzes the history and politicization of the fight for women to access birth control in America.

Debrah Rowland. *Boundaries of Her Body: A Troubling History of Women's Rights in America.* Naperville, IL: Sphinx, 2004. This is a comprehensive guide to the history of women's legal rights in the United States.

Ahmed E. Souaiaia. *Contesting Justice: Women, Islam, Law, and Society.* New York: SUNY Press, 2009. The author examines the relationship between Islam and modern feminism, including issues such as freedom of speech, abortion privacy rights, and others.

Laurel Thatcher Ulrich. *Well Behaved Women Seldom Make History.* New York: Vintage, 2008. This work examines several literary and politically groundbreaking women throughout history and how they advanced women's rights.

Uni Wikan. *In Honor of Fadime: Murder and Shame.* Chicago: University of Chicago Press, 2008. The author examines the honor killing of Fadime Sahindal by her father in Sweden and compares others like it throughout the world.

Periodicals

Sarah Blustain. "The Mourning After," *Nation*, January 17, 2008. www.thenation.com/doc/20080204/blustain.

William John Cox. "Abortion: The Government's Choice? Reproductive Rights in the New America," Global Research, October 27, 2008. www.globalresearch.ca/index.php?context=va&aid=10715.

Danielle Crittenden. "Islamic Like Me: 'Do You Have Sky Miles?'" Huffington Post.com, December 10, 2007. www.huffingtonpost.com/danielle-crittenden/islamic-like-me-do-you-_b_76031.html.

Tommy De Seno. "*Roe vs. Wade* and the Rights of the Father," Fox Forum, January 22, 2009. http://foxforum.blogs.foxnews.com/2009/01/22/deseno_roe_wade/.

Mary Dixon. Testimony of the ACLU of Illinois in Support of Proposed Permanent Rule (68 ILL. ADM. CODE 1330.91 [k]), June 2, 2006. www.acluil.org/legislative/dixontestimony.pdf.

Mona Eltahawy. "Caught in the Clash of Civilizations," *International Herald Tribune*, January 18, 2008. www.iht.com/articles/2008/01/18/opinion/edelta.php.

Sabrina Rubin Erdely. "Could Your Doctor Deny You Healthcare?" *Self*, June 2007. www.self.com/health/2007/05/denial-of-health-care?printable=true.

Linda Feldman. "Hillary Clinton Shattered a Political Glass Ceiling: Despite Some Sexism on the Campaign Trail and in the Media, Her Gender Won Many Votes, Too," *Christian Science Monitor*, June 6, 2008. www.csmonitor.com/2008/0606/p01s04-uspo.html.

Jill Filipovic. "Terminating Women's Rights," April 19, 2007. www.huffingtonpost.com/jill-filipovic/terminating-womens-right_b_46332.html.

Amanda Fortini. "The 'Bitch' and the 'Ditz': How the Year of the Woman Reinforced the Most Pernicious Sexist Stereotypes and Actually Set Women Back," *New York*, November 16, 2008. http://nymag.com/news/politics/nationalinterest/52184/.

Kim Gandy. "Father's Rights . . . and Wrongs," National Organization for Women, Summer 2006. www.now.org/nnt/summer-2006/viewpoint.html.

Michelle Goldberg. "Abortion Rights Go Global," Slate.com, January 29, 2009. www.slate.com/id/2209916/.

Zubin Jelveh. "Affirmative Action for Women Works," Conde Nast Portfolio.com, May 21, 2008. www.portfolio.com/views/blogs/odd-numbers/2008/03/21/affirmative-action-for-women-works.

Jen. "Conscientious Objection: Not Just for the Military Anymore," BrooWaha.com, June 30, 2007. http://losangeles.broowaha.com/article.php?id=1894.

Allison Kaplan. "Cover(ed) Girls," *Knight Ridder-Tribune Business News*, October 14, 2007.

David Koon. "Neither Rebel nor Victim," *Arkansas Times*, September 13, 2007, pp. 14–17.

Nicholas D. Kristof. "When Women Rule," *New York Times*, February 10, 2008. www.nytimes.com/2008/02/10/opinion/10kristof.html.

Dahlia Lithwick. "Martyrs and Pestles," Slate.com, April 13, 2005. www.slate.com/id/2116688/.

Wendy McElroy. "Abortion Bills Violate Men's Rights," Fox News.com, December 12, 2006. www.foxnews.com/story/0,2933,236144,00.html.

Frank A. Pavone. "Abortion: A Choice Against Women," Priests for Life, www.priestsforlife.org/brochures/abortionchoice.html.

Nicholas Provenzo. "The Fundamental Right to Abortion," Center for the Advancement of Capitalism, September 18, 2008. www.moraldefense.com/Philosophy/Commentary/08/09-18-08.htm.

Catherine Rampell. "Political Affirmative Action: Quotas for Women," *New York Times*, January 12, 2009. http://economix.blogs.nytimes.com/2009/01/12/political-affirmative-action-quotas-for-women/.

Stella Ramsaroop. "Why Men Should Have No Say on the Abortion Issue," FeminismOnline.com, May 14, 2005. http://feminism

online.com/2005/05/14/why-men-should-have-no-say-on-the-abortion-issue/.

Jeanne Sahadi. "The 76-Cent Myth: Do Women Make Less than Men?" CNN.com, February 21, 2006. http://money.cnn.com/2006/02/21/commentary/everyday/sahadi/.

Mary Ann Sieghart. "Can't Muslim Men Control Their Urges?" *Times* (London), November 2, 2006. www.freerepublic.com/focus/f-news/1730315/posts.

Stephanie Simon. "Changing Abortion's Pronoun," *Los Angeles Times*, January 7, 2008. www.latimes.com/news/nationworld/nation/la-na-menabort7jan07,0,5749127.story.

Joan Smith. "The Veil . . . and Why These Leading Muslims Won't Wear It," *Independent*, December 31, 2006.

Robert Spencer. "'Unveiled Women Are Like Uncovered Meat,'" *Human Events*, November 6, 2006, p. 12.

Jesse Sposato. "Conservative Muslim Women Hide Knack for Fashion Under Their Religious Robes," *New York Sun*, January 27, 2008. www2.nysun.com/article/70250.

Rob Stein. "'Pro-Life' Drugstores Market Beliefs," *Washington Post*, June 16, 2008. www.washingtonpost.com/wpdyn/content/article/2008/06/15/AR2008061502180.html?hpid=moreheadlines.

Gloria Steinem. "Women Are Never Front-Runners," *New York Times*, January 8, 2008. www.nytimes.com/2008/01/08/opinion/08steinem.html.

Nathan Tabor. "The Third Victim of Abortion," *Intellectual Conservative*, April 15, 2005. www.intellectualconservative.com/article4276.html.

Cathy Young. "A Great Moment for Women," *Reason*, September 17, 2008. www.reason.com/news/show/128836.html.

Web Sites

Abstinence Clearinghouse (www.abstinence.net). The Abstinence Clearinghouse provides information about abstinence programs and education. Its Web site provides hundreds of resources for those seeking to remain abstinent until marriage. It also hosts a blog where authors discuss the impact of society on teens and sexuality.

Islam for Today (www.islamfortoday.com). This site was created by a former Christian living in the West who converted to Islam. It provides information about Islam for those that have also converted to the religion. It addresses several issues, including Muslim women's rights.

Living the Legacy: The Women's Rights Movement, 1848 to 1998 (www.legacy98.org). Living the Legacy is sponsored by the National Women's History Project. Its mission is to educate the public about the history of the fight for women's rights. It provides a history of the women's movement, a detailed time line, issues to watch, and a list of organizations that follow issues that affect women.

The National Women's Health Information Center (www.womens health.gov). This Web site was established by the U.S. Department of Health and Human Services Office of Women's Health to give free access to gender-specific health information to women and girls. Information is available on a wide range of topics, including birth control and emergency contraception.

Women, Power, and Politics—an Online Exhibit (www.imow.org). The International Museum of Women created this site as an online exhibit dedicated to women in politics. It includes a welcome video, online discussion groups, a reference section, and stories of female leaders around the world.

Index

A

Abortion
  is not woman's right, 90–95
  is woman's right, 82–89
  men's feelings about, 96–106
Abortion pill, 84
Afghanistan, 38–40
Africa, 7–9
Ahmadiyya Muslim
  Community, 53
Alcorn, Randy, 90–95
American Association of
  University Women (AAUW),
  19–20
American Islamic Fellowship,
  70
American Medical Association,
  118
American Pharmacist
  Association, 117–118
Amniocentesis, 95
Anthony, Susan B., 93

B

Babbitt, Eileen, 40
Birth control
  failures of, 85
  methods of, 110–111
  is not a right, 115–120
  right to access, 107–114
Blagojevich, Rod, 116
Bodily autonomy, 85–86

Bottcher, Rosemary, 91
Brown, Gordon, 58
Burka, 63, 66–68
Bush, George W., 42

C

Canada, 64
Career
  choices, 13–16, 20–22
  gender and, 33, 35
Carey, Sarah, 107–114
Carroll, Jill, 37–42
Chapman, Steve, 18–23
Chastity, 44–45, 47
Child care, 13–14, 20, 22
China, 95
Civil Rights Act (1964), 16
Clinton, Hillary Rodham,
  25–27, 28
Commission for Equality and
  Human Rights, 32
Contraception. See Birth control
Crittenden, Danielle, 62–68
Cultural tolerance, 63–64

D

Daly, Martin, 108, 109, 112–
  113
Dey, Judy Goldberg, 11–17
Divorce, in Islam, 46–47
Domestic violence, 60, 70,
  72–74, 77, 78

Dworkin, Ronald, 86

E
Education Amendments (1972), 16
El-Sayyed, Alaa, 77
Emergency contraception, 108–109, 112–114
Equal Opportunities Commission (EOC), 31–32
Equal Pay Day, 19
Equal Rights Amendment (ERA), 93

F
Fatherhood, 15–16
Female genital mutilation (FGM), 7–9, 46, 64–66
Feminism
    abortion and, 92–94
    veil as symbol of, 58–60
Feminists for Life, 91, 92, 93
Ferraro, Geraldine, 33
Foster, Serrin, 92
France, 67
Frogh, Wazhma, 38–42
Furedi, Ann, 82–89

G
Gartrell, Gail, 76
Gender inequality, in Muslim world, 38
Gender pay gap
    does not exist, 18–23
    exists, 11–17

Girls
    discrimination against Muslim, 46
    killed by abortions, 95
Glass ceiling, 31, *32*, 35
Goldin, Claudia, 22
Gornick, Vivian, 24–29

H
Harney, Mary, 113
Hassan, Riffat, 43–49
Henderson, Mark, 83
Hijab, 58, 59, 67
    See also Veil
Hill, Catherine, 11–17
Honor killings
    vs. domestic violence, 78
    Islam condemns, 69–74
    Islam condones, 75–80
    Muslim culture and, 45–46, 64, 66
    protests against, *45*
Husbands, Muslim, 46, 48

I
India, 95
Inequality, 26
Islam
    condemns honor killings, 69–74
    condones honor killings, 75–80
    does not respect women's rights, 43–49
    respects women's rights, 37–42

violence against women in name of, 50–54

Islamic law, 53–54, 72

J

Johansen, Jay, 115–120

Jordan, 79

Jordan, Beth, 116

K

Kanwal, Sandela, 70

Koran
  condemns violence, 72
  women's rights in, 44, 46–49, 57–58

Koroma, Hannah, 8

Ku Klux Klan robes, 67

L

Legal system, in Saudi Arabia, 53–54

Levonelle, 112

Linklater, Magnus, 30–35

M

Marriage, 46, 48

Martin, Courtney E., 96–101

McCleary, Rachel, 39–40

Medical abortions, 84

Medical interventions, 85–86

Men
  abortion and, 94, 96–106
  approach to career by, 33, 35
  fatherhood and, 15–16
  work hours of, 22

Michelman, Kate, 91

Moral decisions, 86

Morning-after pill, 108–109, 112–114

Morrow, Mark B., 103

Motherhood, 14–16, *15*, 20

Muslim cultures, 44–48
  See also Islam

N

Nathanson, Bernard, 93

Niger, 9

Nikab, 58, 59, 60

O

Obama, Barack, 27

Occupational choices, 13–16

O'Neill, June, 22

Oral contraceptives, 116
  See also Birth control

P

Pakistan, 72

Palin, Sarah, 25, 27, 33

Parvez, Aqsa, 76–77, *77*

Parvez, Muhammad, 77, 79

Patient's rights, 120

Paul, Alice, *92*, 93

Pelosi, Nancy, 31

Pharmacists, 115–120

Planned Parenthood Federation, 93

Politics
  barriers facing women in, 24–29
  number of women in, 34

women do not face barriers in, 30–35
Polygamy, 47
Price, Catherine, 102–106

Q
Qur'an. *See* Koran

R
Racism, 27
Rape, 53
Reid, John, 58
Religion, power of, 40–41
Religious freedom, 64
Religious police, 51, 53
Ridley, Yvonne, 55–61
Robertson, Pat, 61
Robinson, Melissa, 69–74
Roe v. Wade, 92

S
Said, Amina, 76, 79
Said, Islam, 76
Said, Sarah, 76, 79
Said, Yaser, 76, 79
Sanadzai, Vida, 59
Sanger, Margaret, 93
Saudi Arabia, 51–54
Sex education, 97
Sex-selection abortions, 95
Sexism in politics, 24–29
Shariah law, 53–54, 72
Shostak, Arthur, 99, 100–101, 105
Siddiqui, Shahina, 77
Spencer, Robert, 75–80

Straw, Jack, 56

T
Taliban, 56, 67
Tampka, Kompoa, 9
Turkey, 67

U
United Kingdom, abortion in, 83–89
United States
    female genital mutilation in, 64, 65–66
    honor killings in, 70, 71, 76–77, 79
    support for abortion in, 84

V
Veil
    protects women's rights, 55–61
    in Saudi Arabia, *52*
    violated women's rights, 62–68
Vindication of the Rights of Woman (Wollstonecraft), 27–28
Violence against women
    Islam and, 60
    in name of Islam, 50–54
    in West, 63–66
    See also Domestic violence; Honor killings

W
Wages. *See* Gender pay gap

West, subjugation of women in, 60–61
Wollstonecraft, Mary, 27
Women
   career choices of, 13–16, 20–22
   college-educated, 12–13, 20
   motherhood and, 14–16, 20
   progress made by, 32–33
Women's movement, 27–28
Women's rights
   abortion as, 82–89
   abortion is not, 90–95

Islam does not respect, 43–49
Islam respects, 37–42
in Koran, 44, 46–49, 57–58
status of, 7
veil protects, 55–61
veil violates, 62–68
Workplace discrimination, 16–17
World Health Organization (WHO), 8–9

Z
Zafar, Harris, 50–54

Picture Credits